Crossing
the River

Crossing the River

A NOVEL

Fenton Johnson

A Birch Lane Press Book
Published by Carol Publishing Group

This is a work of fiction. Any similarity of persons, places or events depicted herein to actual persons, places or events is purely coincidental.

Copyright © 1989 by Fenton Johnson

A Birch Lane Press Book
Published by Carol Publishing Group

Editorial Offices
600 Madison Avenue
New York, NY 10022

Sales & Distribution Offices
120 Enterprise Avenue
Secaucus, NJ 07094

In Canada: Musson Book Company
A division of General Publishing Co. Limited
Don Mills, Ontario

All rights reserved. No part of this book
may be reproduced in any form, except by
a newspaper or magazine reviewer who wishes
to quote brief passages in connection
with a review.

Queries regarding rights and permissions
should be addressed to: Carol Publishing Group,
600 Madison Avenue, New York NY 10022

Manufactured in the United States of America

Library of Congress Cataloging-in-Publication Data

Johnson, Fenton.
  Crossing the river : a novel / Fenton Johnson.
  p.   cm.
  "A Birch Lane Press book."
  ISBN   1-55972-000-X : $15.95
  I. Title.
  PS3560.03766C7   1989   89-34206
  813'.54—dc20   CIP

FOR MOTHER AND FATHER
THE BETTER STORYTELLERS

I gratefully acknowledge James A. Michener and the Copernicus Foundation for their financial support in completing the first draft of this novel. Thanks to Susan Luttner for technical support, and to Jerry Johnson for moral support.

* * *

Chapter IV of this novel appeared as a story, "Crossing the River," in the Spring 1984 issue of *Fiction Network* magazine.

Prologue
1944

She With Her Eyebrows
Arched

MARTHA MIRACLE was still Martha Bragg Pickett in 1944, three years out of high school and no more than three generations and several cousins removed from the Confederate general whose name she carried like a flag. He had advanced into Kentucky, General Bragg, had fought his bloody battle at Perryville, and retreated, unaware that the Yankees had fled north and that Frankfort and Louisville and the entire renegade state were his for the taking. Martha was convinced that had she led the charge, the battle would not have been lost.

She had blue eyes and enough red hair that neighbors in Mount Hermon asked where it came from. The Braggs and the Picketts both denied it. When anyone raised the question they ran distraught fingers through their brown hair, and rolled their brown eyes to the sky. "From General Bragg himself?" Martha's mother asked.

The question in her voice gave her away. *She* had no idea where this wild daughter had come from. She had raised a daughter to go to Mount Hermon Baptist Church Sunday school and socials looking for a man, to humor once she'd got him. If she insisted she could do as she pleased, but only behind her husband's back.

With Martha, only the doing as she pleased part stuck. She rode motorcycles and smoked cigarettes and kept company with older men who ought properly to have been in Europe making the world safe for democracy. With girls from less respectable families she sneaked across the river to buy beer from the Catholics.

Her mother held stony silence longer than Job, dropping only darkest hints that the Boatyard Bridge, and those Catholics, would be her daughter's downfall.

Martha's mother was right. One cold March night, after two beers and a dare, Martha Bragg Pickett drove her friend Rosie Uptegrove across the river, to buy a beer and fall in love in the New Hope Miracle Inn.

Crossing the river was nothing new to Martha Pickett. She'd been born to cross borders; there were plenty of borders to cross, in any direction she turned.

In high school she'd had a history teacher from the North, a balding bachelor from Ohio with a liberal education who had proved to her class that by World War II there no longer existed a North and a South. Pulling a mutilated map from a ceiling tube, he'd pointed out that places you'd expect to be South (like Northern Kentucky) were really North, and places you expected to be North (like Southern Indiana and Little Egypt in Illinois) were really South.

This sounded good in class and had the map to support it,

but Martha and everybody else knew the North ended and the South began at the Boatyard Bridge.

Catholics lived in New Hope, north of the bridge. Liquor was legal north of the bridge, all the way north to Louisville along the old Jackson Highway (named after the seventh president of the United States). Living rooms north of the bridge were garnished with pictures of the Pope and the Virgin Mary. Men fought with guns and married late and had big families, a child a year beginning ten months after the wedding. Black women worked cleaning white women's houses and black men hung out at the Standard Station drinking moonshine and smoking and looking for work that never came except during the tobacco harvest.

The Boatyard Bridge separated New Hope and the North from Mount Hermon and the South. Baptists and foot-washing fundamentalists lived in Mount Hermon, Martha's own Pickett clan among them. The town was as dry as September, with no legal alcohol to be had for tears or money all along the Jackson Highway (named after the Confederate general) from Mount Hermon to the Tennessee line. Parlors south of the bridge carried Norman Rockwell cutouts from *The Saturday Evening Post*. Men fought with knives and married young. Their wives had their first baby seven months later, with a single brother or sister to follow. Black women worked cleaning white women's houses, and black men hung out at the Gulf Station and drank moonshine and smoked and looked for work that never came except during the tobacco harvest.

The towns needed an ocean between them but all they had was the Boatyard, a wide riffle in the Knobs Fork River that marked the inland limit of flatboat travel from the Ohio. The first two bridges over the Boatyard burned within a month of being built. The third was blown up a half hour after John Hunt Morgan used it to lead his Confederate Raiders north.

For seventy-four years after, a rickety wooden structure stood, until the Great Flood of 1937 swallowed it whole, along with much of Mount Hermon and New Hope.

That summer, both sides were too occupied with their own miseries to bother with the bridge. Then Franklin Roosevelt solved the problem by declaring the Jackson Highway a federal road and erecting the long narrow webbing of iron girders and concrete pilings and plank flooring, the bridge that on that cold March evening in 1944 carried Martha Pickett and Rosie Uptegrove across the river to the Miracle Inn.

No woman, Catholic or Protestant, white or black, set foot in the Miracle Inn. This fact weighed heavily on Martha as she struck out from the Inn parking lot. Rosie, the coward, stayed quaking in the car.

Inside, Martha tried to ease the door shut. It swung to with a heavy bang. Two men hard at a craps game looked up, into the beveled mirror that backed the liquor bottles for the length of the bar. Bernie Miracle polished glasses, his back to the door.

A twelve-point buck or a federal marshal with his badge displayed might have crossed the room unnoticed. Not a woman. The men swiveled their bodies and stood, backs against the bar, their heels hooked on its brass rail. No one spoke.

Hearing the misstep, Bernie raised his head to the mirror. Between reflections of bottles and backs and his own bony face, he was uncertain of what he saw. He figured, stopped, figured again, turned around, stared.

Martha stood at the opposite end of the bar from the men. "A beer," she said. Her voice squeaked.

Bernie jerked his head towards the men. "Down there," he said.

"What?"

"Leave her where she belongs," one man said. His partner snickered.

14

"I can't serve you there," Bernie said. "That's the colored bar."

"Oh," Martha said. "Sorry."

"You said it honey," the second man said.

Martha moved on frozen feet to the other end of the bar. She forced one foot onto the rail. "A beer," she said, more firmly.

"You ain't serving her where you're serving me," the second man said.

Bernie spread bony hands on the bartop. "Ma'am . . . ."

"No 'ma'am' to her," the second man said. "Get her out."

Bernie wadded the towel in his hands and flipped it onto the bar. A stubborn look came into his eyes that Martha came later to know too well. "I make the rules around here," he said.

"If your father was alive he wouldn't of let her cheap ass past that door," the first man said.

"Since he's dead I guess he don't have much say," Bernie said. "You got money?" Martha fumbled in her purse and put a dime on the counter. "You got your beer."

The men gathered their dice and left. At the door the second spat a wad of tobacco juice on the jamb.

Martha sagged against the bar and sipped her beer. Over the rim of her glass she surveyed the Miracle Inn.

The bar formed a long shallow U, broken by a hinged flap that raised to let the bartender out and that separated colored from white. The white bar was rich brown mahogany, carved in a plain pattern of rectangles and squares. The colored bar was golden oak, supported by pilasters elaborately carved with fruits and vines and clusters of grapes. In its center a sun rose, or set, between wooded hills. Above the beveled mirror hung a large oval daguerreotype of a clean-shaven, square-jawed man, dressed in Union blues. He fixed her with a calm, stubborn stare. Except for his uniform he might have been the

15

twin of the man who stood before her now, rubbing his bartender's towel in furious circles.

Bernie saw her looking up. "My great-grandfather," he said, snapping his towel at the picture. "Built this place. Fought under General Grant and sold whiskey to Confederate soldiers on the side. Not much different now, I guess." From under the bar he pulled an engraved silver flask. "Have a swig," he said. Martha blushed and shook her head. "Go on," he said. "It was his, great-grandfather's. It's not everybody that walks in here gets it offered, I'll tell you *that*."

She closed her eyes and raised the flask to her lips. In the burning clearness that followed, she saw it all plain: pure hellfire, this, that twenty-two years of Baptist preaching had contrived to keep her from. For a single sharp moment, she felt deliriously evil. She took a second swig. "I guess I cost you a couple of customers," she said, to break the silence.

Bernie delicately lifted the flask from her fingers and tucked it under the bar. "Nobody I mind losing. It's good for them to figure out who's boss. They think just because they knew my daddy they got the run of the place."

"I'm sorry he's dead."

"No need," he said cheerfully. He ducked under the flap and leaned next to her, too close. "He was a Miracle. Live hard, die young. He got what was coming to him. They found him floating in the river out back, the day Prohibition ended. 'Stroke,' the coroner said, 'swhat done it, but in these parts pretty much anything that's not done by a car or a gun they call a stroke."

"I think I'd best be going," Martha said. "I don't want to cost you any more business."

"How come so soon? You just got here." Bernie cocked his head in a sideways stare.

16

"Somebody's waiting," she said, thankful it was true.

"Suit yourself. Next time bring your friend in."

She stepped away carefully, watching the floor for cracks in the planking. When she reached the door he was there. "You didn't tell me your name," he said. "Surely for the price of two customers I get to meet the first girl to set foot in the Miracle Inn."

"Will you let me out."

"Sure. I'm just being social. That's a bartender's job."

She looked him over carefully. She knew who *he* was, of course, but if she hadn't anyone with open eyes could spot a Miracle a mile away: a hawk's nose, big brown eyes, a jaw formed with a T-square, framing a wide mouth with horses' teeth the color of grits. Taken one by one his features were mismatched but as a whole they fit together in a way that was engaging, if the light wasn't too good.

The light was dim enough that night in the doorway of the Miracle Inn. Martha felt the full weight of twenty-two unmarried years in Mount Hermon, with a mother who smelled sin any time the wind blew from across the river and with Rosie Uptegrove, her best friend, already married two years. Martha risked a second glance. In the half light she thought she saw blond lights in his hair—just a few. She was a sucker for blonds. "Martha," she said. "Martha Bragg Pickett."

His arm dropped. "I'll be damn," he said. "I thought you looked familiar. You're from across the river." She fled.

* * *

His invitation arrived two weeks later. It carried a New Hope postmark, and was scrawled in a hand as spindly and angular as Bernie himself.

March 14, 1944

Dear Miss Martha Bragg Pickett,

I would appreciate the honor of taking you to next Sunday
Mass. I know you are not a Catholic but that is OK by me if it
is OK by you. Please answer to the Miracle Inn, Jackson
Highway, New Hope.

Sincerely,
Francis Bernard Miracle

She'd got the letter not in the mail but from Ossetta, the
black woman who cleaned houses on both sides of the
river. Ossetta gave it to Martha out behind the wild cherry
trees, where the two of them were hanging out the day's
wash.

Martha tapped the envelope on Ossetta's shoulder. "Where
did you get this."

Ossetta stuck two clothespins in the corner of her mouth.
"Found it," she said, through the pins.

"With a postmark?"

"Mailman must of dropped it."

Martha held the envelope to the sun. "There's not a speck
of dirt on here."

With a loud snap Ossetta shook the wrinkles from a shirt.
She plucked the pins from her mouth, pinning at the shirt
seams and smoothing the material with a last pat of her palm.
"I got butter to tend to," she said. She stumped toward the
house, trailing the faint odor of garlic. Under the tall straight
trunks of the wild cherries she turned. "You want your mamma to find that, you just let me know. You just let me know. I
let it be."

Martha stood under the spring green buds of the cherry
trees, tapping the envelope's sharp corner into her palm. She

18

had never been inside a Catholic church. She had never dated a Catholic man, much less a man from a family that made a living selling liquor and (if her mother's tales were to be believed) bootlegging south to the dry counties.

She considered exactly one minute. She would go, in secret and in style.

*   *   *

A week later she was at her first Mass.

It was the fourth Sunday in Lent. Martha told her mother she had a headache and lay piled under blankets until her family left for Sunday school. Then she wriggled into her best blouse and stood at the window, pressing Kleenexes to her armpits and waiting for Bernie to drive by and honk, his signal to meet in the back alley.

At Assumption Church she balked, until Bernie slammed the car door and stalked in alone. He thought she was scared. She was terrified, but she wanted to do this alone. She had always been one to do things alone. She had entered the Inn alone. She would enter this church alone, Bernie Miracle or no.

When the church doors had cleared and she was certain the service must be underway, she slipped up the steps. In the vestibule she bent to peer through the single clear pane where the inside doors' stained glass had been broken and replaced.

A marble altar gilt in gold and inlaid with mosaic spanned the nave. Ranged above and around it were figures swathed in purple. She decided they were mummies, saints embalmed until ritual called for their unwinding. In the midst of these gloomy figures the priest stood, dressed in bright pink, his arms raised and his back to the people. He mumbled in what she took to be Latin. The congregation responded in the same

19

spiritless and haphazard mumbling. She heard no organ, though the pipes ranged behind the altar in polished brass splendor. The whole affair seemed ragged around the edges compared to the tidy services at Mount Hermon Baptist Church.

But incense and mystery filled the air. The vestibule smelled faintly of it, a smell she began then to associate with things Catholic. The silence, the enshrouded figures, the priest in pink, the smell of the place, all promised mystery, something under the surface and larger than life: exotic, mysterious, *deep*.

When Mass was over she met Bernie on the steps. She had never touched him before; she seized his arm now, in full view of the stares of all Assumption Church. "What was that all about? I want to know."

With sideways glances Bernie edged her down the stairs. It was one thing to flirt alone, in the Miracle Inn. It was another to display yourself on the church steps, before half the town and all his family. He pulled her towards the car. "What was what about?"

"Church. The Mass. Does he always wear pink? Is that how you talk Latin? Who are the mummies?"

Bernie stopped dead. "Mummies?"

"In purple."

"Oh. The statues."

Martha's jaw dropped. "You dress up *statues*?"

"Well, it's Lent, see."

"That doesn't explain dressing up statues."

"You just *do*, that's all," Bernie said. "Everybody does. Every year. Something about being sorry."

"*They're* sorry?"

"*We're* sorry."

"So you dress them up."

20

"It's not *dressing* them up," Bernie said impatiently. "It's *covering* them up."

"Oh." Martha sensed she'd gone too far. She bit her lip. Bernie glanced about, then patted her hand. She risked another question. "But I don't understand—"

"You're not supposed to understand. You just do it, that's all. That's what religion is about." There was an unmistakable note of finality in his voice.

Martha settled into herself. That wasn't what *her* religion was about, but after twenty-two years of the Mount Hermon Baptist Church and its socials she was ready for something she didn't understand. Bernie's explanation was enough, for now. It seemed like her kind of church, incense and pink cloth and mystery.

And here she was, walking with Bernie Miracle, a man who made his living selling demon rum. She felt a hundred pairs of eyes following them down the walk. *This* was life, she thought. This was love. She squeezed his hand, and smiled when he looked into her eyes.

For the next week she mulled these things over. Bernie Miracle was the most exotic man she'd met. The inside of the Catholic church was the least understandable place she'd been. By the end of the week she'd built a vision of them both, Bernie in a cutaway and herself dressed in white, stepping to the marble altar and saying their vows in Latin, to the dismay of the Pickett clan and the horror of Mount Hermon.

Their courtship set the tongues of Jessup County wagging, distressing Bernie no end until he saw that business at the Inn was actually picking up. For every diehard whose business he lost, he gained two paying customers who couldn't resist the lure of good gossip.

Martha had never been courted by a Catholic. Later she thought she should have seen the problems coming, but at the

21

time she figured this was how they did it, north of the river. It was new and different and she loved it for that. She loved Bernie for that.

He courted her in the family mausoleum, built three generations before by the great-grandfather whose portrait stared down from the Miracle Inn wall. It was a big Tennessee marble cube, that crowned the highest knoll in the cemetery, looking west over the valley to the broad wooded flank of Strang Knob. Its rusting gates of iron filigree led inside, to a small dark room with a single bench. In front, flush with the earth, she saw the names of three generations of Miracles carved into flat, polished granite gravestones. Next to their names were the names of their spouses and children, living and dead, patiently in attendance.

Surely, she thought later, *that* should have told her something. But she was in love: meeting on the sly, in the dark, under the Catholic cemetery's greening persimmon trees, she was in love, for many reasons. Bernie was one of them.

Martha would have had her way, with a wedding as big as Jessup County had seen, but she discovered that no one acknowledged that she was marrying. On both sides of the river she might well have dropped from the face of the social earth. When three months later she said her vows in English, she wore the same plaid blue suit and black-and-white spectator pumps she'd worn to her first Mass.

No one from her family attended. At the last minute Rosie Uptegrove agreed to stand as witness. She sobbed so loudly through the Mass that Martha almost turned around to tell her to shut up. Of Bernie's enormous family, only his youngest brother Leo came, pressed into service as the second witness. He scowled so fiercely when Martha offered her cheek that she pretended she was adjusting her hat.

The priest took the single picture. Rosie and Leo stood

22

stiffly to either side, looking not into the camera but at some point in the far distance. As the priest bent his head to the viewfinder, Martha clutched at the tips of Bernie's fingers. He turned his head towards her. She arched her eyebrows; he gave a broad wink.

PART ONE

Done With Smoke and Mirrors
1967

CHAPTER I

Genealogy

IN MAY of 1967, Martha Pickett Miracle turned forty-five. That same month, her son Miracle graduated from New Hope's Assumption High, only a year late—not bad, Martha figured, for the only heir to the Miracle name. Through high school, at Bernie's insistence, Miracle had worked evenings and weekends at the Miracle Inn—not the easiest place to do homework.

Martha planned a graduation picnic for Miracle, the afternoon of the ceremony. A day earlier, she was laying in a store of fried chicken, a blue bandana wrapped neatly around her red hair, when Miracle came home with the news that their names had been carved into a new gravestone in front of the Miracle mausoleum.

At first Martha thought she'd misheard. She laid her spatula on the stove top and drooped in an undignified slump against the oven. "Straighten up," she said to her son. "You stand like that, you'll grow up to be a hunchback."

A stubborn hardness came into his eyes. "For God's sake, Mother, I *am* grown up. If I was going to be a hunchback it would have happened by now."

Martha straightened. He was grown, no doubt about it, and while his hair had turned brighter red than her own, his jaw stayed as Miracle square as ever. It seemed impossible that her child could have become a man without her taking note of it, but across twenty-three years of marriage to Bernie Miracle she had settled into the habit of daydreaming. Life around New Hope passed her by, without her much remarking on it. More than once Grandma Miracle had startled her from a walking sleep, and blunt Rosie Uptegrove had asked outright if she had taken to drink.

"I'm getting old, I forget these things," Martha said. "Now what are you saying about a tombstone?"

"We're on it, you and me. And Father. There's a new one, pink and flat. Set in the ground in front of the mausoleum."

"The *Miracle* mausoleum?"

"Come on, Mother, what other mausoleum is there?"

Martha jerked the bandana from her head. "This I have to see." She pushed Miracle ahead of her. "So help me, if you're telling a *lie*, Miracle—"

Miracle sidestepped her shove. "Father's got me on a beer run south. Besides, what's the big deal? It's all in the family, is what Father'll say."

"*Your* family. Not mine." Martha pushed out the door, leaving the screen door to slam behind her.

She walked along the Jackson Highway to the cemetery. In the glare of an early summer sun the asphalt shimmered and pooled. Along the river the trees gave off a dusty green haze. On these sorts of days Martha dreamed of being elsewhere, north or in the mountains, someplace where the sun stayed low and you could walk a half mile without getting lightheaded.

She walked down the cemetery drive, beneath persimmons that twenty-three years earlier had lifted limbs over her courting. At the mausoleum she pulled open the filigreed iron gates and sat on the bench inside, thankful to escape the sun for its clammy coolness.

She shaded her eyes against the blinding square of summer sun that beat through the mausoleum gate. Outside she saw the old gravestones, sunk flush with the earth, with three generations of Miracle names carved into their broad granite tops. Next to them was a new stone, one Martha had never seen, a pink granite slab carved with a weeping angel and the names of Bernie's father, long since dumped in the river, and Grandma Miracle, with a blank space left for her date of death. Below those names were carved the names of Bernie's brothers and sisters, each with the birth year followed by a blank. After each Miracle child's name came the name of the wife or husband; under each couple were carved the names of their children, with empty lines allowed for expanding families.

Heading the list, first under Grandma Miracle and her dead husband, came Bernie, their oldest son. Next to Bernie's name she saw her own, and their son's:

FRANCIS BERNARD MIRACLE   1910—
MARTHA PICKETT MIRACLE   1922—
MICHAEL PICKETT MIRACLE   1948—

There were no extra lines below their names.

Martha slumped against the mausoleum wall and took her head in her hands. She was drowning in this family, that divided the world into two camps: for or against, Miracle or no. Like a drowning woman, the more she struggled against the sea around her the more it swallowed her up, flooding her lungs and heart and blood.

She had married Bernie Miracle at a time when marriages did not fail, especially in Kentucky, especially between Catholics. Both families made that clear, though they gave them precious little help elsewhere. She'd married with no more thought of what freedom meant than a cardinal or a whitetail deer might have. Then she found herself alone, with a man who wanted children, as many as a cottontail and the sooner the better.

To Bernie Miracle romance was a necessary but temporary affliction, like Sunday sermons or Republicans in the statehouse. A month after his wedding he'd sloughed it off as surely as a snake's summer molting. He was older than his wife, more than twelve years older. When in those first months after they'd married she fixed him with her steady blue gaze after dinner or before weekday suppers, he was likely to drop what he was doing and make for the refuge of the Miracle Inn. He saw romance as foolishness, over a pleasure meant more for men than for women and more for making babies than for pleasure at all. In those first few months he followed his wife into the bedroom, only to have a neighbor knock or Leo call from the Inn. Bernie would leap from his bed, tugging at his trousers, to realize that at two p.m. there was only one excuse for looking like he'd just jumped from bed. It was not an excuse he was willing to give.

He was too old and too set in his ways for such nonsense. A Sunday came when he plucked Martha's hands from his shoulders. "On a Sunday afternoon," he snorted. "I'll be at the Inn, cleaning up."

Months passed, and a year or two, and Martha Pickett found herself more and more alone. Her conversion angered the Baptists, who turned away if they saw her approaching on the street. Her enthusiasm for her new religion embarrassed the Catholics, who nodded knowingly to each other and waited for her to yield to the prevailing lethargy. On both sides of the river she became a fixture, like the furniture, acknowledged but not necessarily given the time of day.

Had Martha's child arrived sooner, things might have been different. When years passed without a child, Bernie grew exasperated, then resigned. He settled back into the bog of his habits: work at the Inn, work in the garden, work all day, work at night.

Almost four years after they'd married, their son Michael Miracle arrived on the scene. Martha hoped that with a son things would grow better; instead they grew worse. First she and Bernie fought over what to name him; then they fought over what to call him.

Their fights stopped short of shouting, because always Martha gave way. She was not afraid of Bernie; she was afraid of herself. She knew her own fear, she felt the same fear in Bernie: One word too many and this fragile thing between them might shatter. Then where would they be? Alone with the I-told-you-so's of both sides of the river. So she gave way, again and again, until the night when they fought over how many children were to follow this first son.

Martha had tucked their son into his crib, while Bernie watched from their bed, propped on thin elbows. When she climbed into bed, he put a callused hand on her breast. She shivered and drew away. "Don't, Bernie," she said.

"It's been long enough since Miracle was born," Bernie said. "I asked the doctor."

"Not now," she said. "Later."

"Why not now?"

"Because I say why not, that's why not," she said. "Now go to sleep and let me be." She turned out the fringed lamp

31

that hung at the side of their bed. He reached over her shoulder and turned it on. "I say now," he said.

"And I say no."

"Why not."

"Because I'm at my time, if you must know."

"That don't make no difference to me."

"I don't mean that kind of time," Martha said. Her face matched the rose shade that covered the lamp.

"Well what other kind of time is there," Bernie said, propping himself on one elbow. "Making time? That's what I'm interested in." He nestled a cold hand between her thighs.

She pushed his hands away. She searched for words that said what she wanted to say, but if they existed she had not heard them or could not put them together in a way that she could bring herself to say. She had been a wild woman, wild enough to marry a Catholic and cross the river, but she was a lady, raised in a substantial, Baptist family. Wherever she'd dreamed of going when she met Bernie in the back alley that Sunday in Lent, it was not here, married to a man who cared more about his family's precious tavern than about his wife. "There's times, and *times*," she said finally. "Times for babies and times not for babies."

"So? We'll have another baby."

"We can't afford it."

Bernie sat up, folding his arms. "I'm the one who says what we can afford around here."

Martha turned her back. She lay silent, facing the wall, until Bernie grabbed her shoulder and turned her over. "I don't want another baby," she said.

She might have asked for a divorce, or told him she was leaving the Church, or that the Miracle Inn had burned. His square jaw opened and his big eyes were so surprised and hurt that Martha laid a hand on his arm. He shook it off. "You got to," he said. "The *Church* says you got to."

"The Church says we have to—lay together," Martha said. "It doesn't say we have to have sixteen babies."

He slapped her, hard. The baby began to cry. Martha jumped from the bed and ran to the crib, where she clutched the baby to her.

"My mother had ten children and raised every last one that lived to be good, decent human beings," he said. "I hope by God to do the same."

"You can do it with somebody else. One of those Catholic women that's raised to breed."

His eyes closed and when they opened the hurt and surprise were gone. In their place was the hard stubbornness she'd seen before, that night at the Miracle Inn, when he'd watched his customers gather their dice to leave, and in her fights with Bernie over their son's name. With the baby in her arms, she ran into the warm June night. Bernie did not follow.

Since that argument, Bernie might have known her six years or sixty. Twice a year he bought her presents, on Christmas Day and Mother's Day, when the ads in the *Argus* reminded him that presents were expected. On those days he walked to Estill Mallory's and got the key to Mallory's Merchandise from where he knew Estill kept it, on a nail above his gun closet. Bernie opened the store, where he chose a pair of nylon stockings and a useful gadget, a butcher knife or a can opener or whatever caught his eye. He scrawled a note to Estill (*Pls chg 1 pr stockings and 1 bx Msn jrs to my acct Bernie*), locked the store and returned the key. Martha would find the note tucked in the next month's grocery bills. Her birthday, being unadvertised, he forgot.

Once a month they lay together on a day chosen by Martha and signaled by her locking the bedroom door. His thin hips jerked with passion but it was over quickly and just as quickly Martha rose to douche and don her nightgown.

He came to know her schedule as well as she but he never spoke in anticipation or in passion or in aftermath. She hated lying with him for the risk she ran in getting pregnant and she hated her coldness. She tried to make herself enjoy him but when he came at her naked and bony and hard her eyes closed and she saw only the look in his eyes when he refused her her right to be herself, a person apart from the wife of the owner of the Miracle Inn.

Sitting in the Miracle mausoleum, resting her head against the damp marble, Martha wondered why it was they had done this crazy thing. True love and a measure of plain old horniness, she supposed. Two healthy people in heat, that was all. Add a little rambunctiousness (herself) and a fine-tuned will to self-destruct (Bernie). Nothing new under the sun.

Then why couldn't it be undone? The question came to Martha now, and once more she pushed it down and back. She'd pushed it down so hard and so often that soon enough it came only on those hot, breathless, tired days like this one. What's done was done, she'd told herself. After that, you do what you have to do. And what she had to do, what she had *chosen* to do against all advice, was to be the wife of the oldest son of the New Hope Miracles, wife of the owner of the Miracle Inn.

For months after their son was born, Martha had tried calling him Michael, his Christian name, but to no avail. Once it became clear there would be no more Miracles to follow, the town sided with Bernie. Their son became just plain Miracle.

For the five years after his birth, Miracle broke the habits of their lives, or at least of Martha's life. Then school started, and he was gone, leaving Martha alone.

She settled into a pattern as certain as death and regular as the Angelus rung from the squat brick belltower of Assumption Church. She rose at six, to get Bernie off to the Inn by six-thirty, so he could greet the men who stopped at the Inn to buy six-packs of beer for the drive to factories in Louisville or jobs at Fort Knox, a winding one-hour drive to the west. At six-thirty Martha fixed a cup of Maxwell House while Earl Nightingale preached from the radio. At seven Miracle rose to go to school. She fixed him breakfast and saw him to the door. Then her morning, which went by fast enough, between cleaning and gardening and chopping wood.

With the noon Angelus, Bernie came home for a sandwich and a beer. Martha longed to return with him to the Inn, not for his company but for the pleasure of belonging, in some small way, to the world she'd once raced around with such abandon. She watched him go without a word.

Leaning against the doorjamb, watching Bernie go, she thought back to the rambunctious high school girl she'd been. She tried to puzzle out why she'd turned down any number of Baptist tobacco farmers to marry this ornery Catholic from across the river. The sun sank, Miracle was home from school, it was time to fix supper, and she'd found no answers, other than the heat of plain foolish love, a heat she no longer felt.

Faced with the same problems, many of her women friends quietly took to drink. Other women, the no-count women of the hills and hollows, found their way to the far side of Strang Knob, to the ready love of some soldier stationed for a long year at Fort Knox. Every few months Rosie came across the river with tales of another hillbilly woman destroyed by love.

Martha never repeated that sort of gossip. Probably the same thing had been said about her, after she'd married Bernie Miracle. On afternoons like these, fuming uselessly in the Miracle mausoleum, Martha was not sure that what they'd said wasn't true.

She wondered how these lost women had met the men who'd destroyed them; what moment of weakness (or strength?) had possessed these women to betray their husbands; how the couple managed to rendezvous, how the woman (who certainly knew better, whatever her upbringing) had decided that *this* man was different from the man she'd married, and from the housebreakers and heartbreakers she'd been warned against. No doubt these women, whom Rosie Uptegrove called "cheap" and "destroyed by love," had done something like what Martha herself had done, that cold March evening when she'd left her friends and her family and her religion and her town, to strike across the ragged planks of the Miracle Inn, to meet and marry Bernie Miracle.

Of all her mistakes, Martha was determined not to let that one happen again. She'd defied her family, changed her religion, given herself over once to love. Once was quite enough, thank you. Never again would she make a fool of herself for love.

Sitting in the mausoleum, thinking on those women, thinking over her years with Bernie, Martha understood why they left everything they knew, to go against their own. Not from love—surely any woman who had been in love knew how little that was worth, and what it came to. They left instead because of their dreams, that things could be better, that this man might offer a way out: out of town, out of marriage, out of this life. That was the only chance worth taking.

But where they had left, she had stayed, Martha Pickett Miracle; from duty, from love for her son, for the sake of the love—she knew no other word for it—that had first brought her across the river.

In staying, she fought back. She had to, if only to prove to herself that she was still alive. She gathered herself up now from the mausoleum's cold marble bench, dusting the spiderwebs from her hair with the bandana she'd brought from home. She stepped outside, to stand in the sun, looking over the mausoleum stones; reading her own name engraved in pink granite, until her fury returned. Then she stormed up the cemetery drive and across town to the Miracle Inn, switching the bandana back and forth like a flag.

Inside the Inn, she tossed the bandana on the bartop. "I won't stand for it," she said.

Bernie was alone. The farmers were in the fields, the commuters off to work, the Fort Knox soldiers who brought the Inn much of its business were on the firing ranges to the west. He took a towel from below the bar and began rubbing its mahogany surface in deliberate circles. "Stand for what," he said.

"Having my name carved on a grave forty years before I'm dead. Fifty years. It's—morbid, that's what it is. Tempting fate."

Bernie pulled his hair taut against his skull. He plucked at his elbows and lit a cigarette and drummed the bartop with his fingers. "We've done it for years. The only reason we hadn't done it before is because I hadn't had the money. The Miracles always do it. List the family all together. Great-grandpa Miracle started it, said it gave him comfort to know he was going to be buried with the family."

"It gives me the creeps."

"You can live with the creeps. Don't the family mean anything to you?" Bernie's hands danced across the bartop, wiping at invisible spills and years-old water spots. "I'm twelve years older than you, Martha Miracle. Who's to say it don't give me some comfort, knowing I'm to be buried with my family. Would you rather leave your name off? All my brothers and sisters there, with their wives and husbands and kids, and me by myself?"

37

"You're damn straight. That's exactly what I'd want, if that's what it came to."

Bernie flushed bright red. He worried the towel in his hands. "This family don't mean a thing to you," he said in a low voice. "You been part of it for over twenty years and it don't mean beans to you. You use the name but you might as well call yourself Mallory, or Skaggs, or Pickett, or any other name that takes your liking. Look around you," he said, waving the towel at the empty Inn. "This place has been in the family longer than you or me. That mausoleum has carried our name longer than you or me. God and my son willing both the mausoleum and the Inn will carry the Miracle name after we're gone."

"Not if I can help it," Martha said, but she muttered that into the beveled mirror behind the bar.

For the convenience of Baptist farmers too shy to come inside, Bernie had installed a driveup window, and now its buzzer rang. While he waited on his customer, Martha tried to calm her racing heart. When he returned, she spoke in an even voice. "I understand why you wanted to include me, and I'm . . . I'm touched. But you could have asked. Surely."

"Don't need to ask. You're my wife. You're family, ain't you?"

Martha snatched the towel from his astonished hands. She searched the room for a target. She threw it at Bernie's great-grandfather, staring from above the bar. "Damn the family!" she cried. "You have my name taken off that stone or I'll take a hammer and chisel and take it off myself!"

Bernie walked the length of the mahogany bar, picked up the towel from where it had fallen, folded it in a neat square. When he returned the color was gone from his cheeks, leaving them so white that every pore and scar stood out in relief. His eyes were glazed with stubbornness. "You do that," he said, simply and quietly, "and you'll be no wife of mine."

They glared across the bar. Through the bottles of bourbon and gin and vodka Martha found she was glaring at her own reflection. Her red hair tumbled wildly about, and in her blue Pickett eyes she saw a look she had never seen, not in herself: a stubbornness she'd learned from Bernie, the same hardness that set Bernie's chin and filled his eyes.

She dropped her eyes and stepped back. For more than twenty years she'd talked past this man, while he talked past her. As her son grew older and she grew older she found that worked less and less. There was no time for these games, the dodging and feinting and I-said-this, no-you-said-that. She was forty-five and growing older, *old*. The truth took long enough, God knows, without lies to complicate it. And yet here they were. Should she say something, break this thing open right here and now, in the Miracle Inn, under Bernie's great-grandfather's smile?

She took the bandana from the bar. With a great effort she lifted her eyes. "I'm sorry I threw the towel," she said. "Leave the tombstone the way it is. I'll pretend it's not there." She left the Inn, tripping blindly over the uneven floorboards.

CHAPTER II

Picnic

THE NEXT DAY, Martha threw her graduation picnic for Miracle, and the Great Society sent a blond Yankee to rebuild the Boatyard Bridge.

Planning Miracle's picnic was no easy job. It was important to find neutral ground, someplace where both the Picketts and the Miracles could appear without losing face. North of the bridge was out—too far from Pickett territory. But Bernie and the rest of the Miracles never ventured south of the bridge except to bootleg. Martha considered, half-seriously, floating her picnic in the Knobs Fork River, the only place she knew that was neither Catholic nor Baptist, Miracle nor Pickett, North nor South.

In the shadow of the south levee, under the pilings of the Boatyard Bridge, Mount Hermon had mowed the smartweed, cleared the cows, and hung a sign reading *Boatyard Park*. It was the closest thing to a demilitarized zone Martha could find. She held the graduation picnic there.

She invited them all, Bernie's family and her own and Bernie's friends. Of her Baptist friends from her childhood in Mount Hermon, she invited only Willie and Rosie Uptegrove, and their children, Bradford and Rosamund. From Ossetta, Martha had learned that her son Miracle had been mooning over Rosamund. Martha disliked Rosamund, and suspected that if asked Rosie Uptegrove would say the same about Miracle. Still, it was Miracle's party. If he wanted Rosamund Uptegrove there, Martha would extend the invitation.

Bernie saw her invitation list, scrawled across the back of a Campbell's soup label. "You'll never get them all there," he said. "My mother wouldn't sit at the same table as your mother for all the gold in Fort Knox."

"She'll sit at the same table or she won't come," Martha said. "I refuse to argue about it." They seldom argued about anything these days, but Martha took pleasure in refusing her husband the chance. She refused him everything she could manage, within the bounds of politeness and a reasonable honoring of her marriage bond. After all, when it mattered he had refused her, out of nothing more than that Miracle insistence on doing things the way the family, *his* family, had always done them. "I've never known a Baptist to turn down free food or a Catholic to turn down free liquor and there'll be both," she said. "You just keep the Catholics out of the river and the booze in paper cups, that's all I ask. You'll do everybody a favor and leave the Baptists to me. *I* grew up with them."

She sent Miracle ahead early, to meet Ossetta and figure out who would be sitting where. Ossetta was short and thick, the color of vanilla extract, and wore a nylon stocking over her hair when she worked for white folks. Always she trailed the faint odor of garlic and asafetida she wore wrapped in a cheesecloth at her throat to ward off germs and evil spirits.

41

The Knobs Fork River was small, but the bottoms were swampy and the bridge was long, eight sections of webbed iron girders supporting a one-lane oak-planked roadway soaked in creosote. The road ran along a levee a half-mile to the towns on either side. The levee was so narrow the highway department built turnarounds, little tabs of land where farmers meeting in pickups could pull in their side mirrors, crank down their windows and chat. Ossetta and Miracle met on the south levee, at the last of the turnarounds, overlooking the park. Together they surveyed the field.

Ossetta shook her head. "There ain't enough room," she said. "There ain't a flat spot big enough in all Jessup County to hold the Picketts and the Miracles but if there is this ain't it." She pointed to a sassafras bush in the far corner of the field. "Put the beer over there," she said. She pointed to the opposite corner, where a water maple whose trunk the cows had gnawed bare raised scrawny limbs. "And put the table over there. And go back home and get a chair for your Grandma Miracle."

"She's not that old," Miracle said. "She can sit at the table like everybody else."

"I'm not saying she *cain't*," Ossetta said. "I'm saying she *won't*."

By the time Miracle had returned with Bernie and Martha and a chair, nearly everyone had arrived. Scattered at picnic tables close by the river sat most of the Miracle clan: uncles and cousins, aunts and in-laws, nieces and nephews, great-grandchildren still in diapers. Closer to the center of the field the guests of honor were putting up a good show of peace.

Martha sat with Rosie Uptegrove, called Big Rosie now, to set her apart from her daughter Rosamund and for more substantial reasons having to do with an imposing figure and a sharp tongue. She'd been virtuous enough that evening she

42

dared Martha to buy a beer at the Inn—a clean Baptist, and dry as a soda cracker. Since then she'd grown older, bought a television, and grown wiser about the world. She cursed now, whenever it suited her ends. She carried vodka in a half-pint flask designed to look like a makeup kit. When no family were looking, she tipped little splashes into her soft drinks, with a sly wink to anybody who might happen to see.

Next to Martha and Big Rosie Uptegrove sat Dolores Miracle, a frayed woman with hair the color and texture of binder twine. She spent much of her life agreeing with her husband Leo, Bernie's youngest brother. Leo was sitting across from the three women. When Big Rosie laughed or waved her hands or said something in capital letters, the table tilted and Leo seesawed in the air.

At the head of the table Martha's mother Mrs. R. J. Pickett sat in a wicker chair, puckering her nose as if sin were hanging there for the smell. She was a thin, sharp-chinned woman whose concession to vice was bridge club on alternate Tuesdays. She hadn't approved of her daughter's marriage twenty-three years before; she saw no reason to start now.

As far from Mrs. Pickett as Ossetta could manage sat Bernie's mother, Grandma Miracle. She was a wiry woman whose cotton print dresses sank into her concave chest, and whose jaw kneaded a pinch of snuff tucked in her left cheek. She had raised a family on the edge of wilderness and herded them every Sunday to Mass, no matter what the weather. She had not held them together through Prohibition and bootlegging and her husband's death to see them marry Baptists from across the river.

Miracle was heading towards his Grandmother Pickett with his respects and a cup of Nehi Orange when he spotted Rosamund Uptegrove. She sat sideways to him, in a scarlet two-piece bathing suit too tight to have come from any place in

43

Jessup County. She was threading white clover blossoms in a chain, and when she leaned over to pick a flower her hair fell across her shoulder and lay black against skin that shone pale white as if lit from inside. She hummed a Patsy Cline tune as she picked.

Miracle coughed and shifted the Nehi from one hand to another. Rosamund never lifted her eyes but kept searching for clover blossoms as if they were meant to feed the starving children of India. Then she stood, stretching white arms against the startled blue sky. Her breasts strained against her suit. She turned and walked to the river on long legs. With each step her hips wrinkled the bottom of her suit.

"Miracle, if you crane your neck an inch further you'll get a crick and be walking sideways when you take your diploma," Grandmother Pickett said. "Not that I blame him," she said to the sky. "Any girl in an outfit like that is asking for whatever she gets."

"That outfit came all the way from Lexington," Big Rosie Uptegrove said, "And I think it's real sharp. A girl's got to keep up with the styles if she's going to get her a man."

"I hadn't seen a man in Jessup County that knew the difference between styles ten years ago and styles ten years from now," Grandmother Pickett said.

"You're assuming she wants a man from Jessup County to notice what she's got," Big Rosie said. She jabbed a finger at Grandmother Pickett. The table tilted upward. Miracle sat to keep his Uncle Leo landbound. "There are bigger fish floating around, a whole ocean of them the far side of Strang Knob. I don't see why a girl with looks and talent and ambition needs to restrict herself to what happens to wash up at her back door." Miracle winced.

Bradford Uptegrove trotted up then, like a muskrat fresh from the water, his thick hair slicked flat over his head and chest and arms. Behind his mother's back he opened a beer without so much as a pop and poured it in a paper cup. Rosamund crossed the field to stand beside him, her head tilted, brushing her hair in long, smooth runs. She lifted the cup from her brother's hand and sat at the far end of the table from Miracle, humming the Patsy Cline tune in time with her brush strokes.

Bradford poured a second beer and walked to the river. He sat next to a girl Miracle had never seen, a pale, moon-faced child who looked a good deal younger than Miracle himself. She had been sitting quietly with her back to the picnic table. For some months Bradford Uptegrove had dated LaHoma Dean Hawkins, a quiet Cumberland Presbyterian from back in the knobs. Miracle guessed that this was that girl, and from the shy hunch in her shoulders he guessed that she had never been among boisterous Catholics who drank and cursed in the light of day.

The table was quiet except for Rosamund's thin hum and an occasional rumble from the Fort Knox firing ranges, just to the west, behind the limestone flank of Strang Knob. With the war in Vietnam, the bombing on the practice ranges had increased. These days it was as familiar a part of their lives as birdsongs or the cattle lowing.

Bradford was the first to break the calm. He jumped up from beside LaHoma Dean and crossed to the picnic table. "Miracle!" he said, sticking out his hand. "Shake the hand of a man that's on his way!"

"We're celebrating ourselves," Big Rosie said. All heads turned. "I don't suppose you've heard, but it'll be in next week's *Argus* anyway. They're rebuilding the Boatyard Bridge!"

"Who's rebuilding," Leo said. He was as thin as his brother Bernie had once been, with a shock of gray hair pasted flat against his skull in front, but springing up behind like a rooster comb.

"The government, of course," Big Rosie said. "Who else builds around here?"

"Government this, government that," Leo said. "Nobody notices nothing wrong with the old bridge until some jackass from Frankfort decides we got to have new bridges."

"I'll thank you to watch your tongue where there's ladies present," Grandmother Pickett said.

"Jesus rode a jackass," Grandma Miracle said.

Grandmother Pickett sniffed. "In *my* Bible he rode a mule."

"Anybody that's ever *rid* a jackass would call it nothing more polite and a good number of things worse," Grandma Miracle said. She leaned over to drop a wad of juice in her can. "Cuss all you want, son," she said. "*I* don't mind."

"Bradford Uptegrove is hiring on," Big Rosie said. "At $10,000 a year and two weeks' paid vacation!"

"Just goes to show it depends on who you know," Leo said.

"We don't know anybody," Big Rosie said. "He got that job because he worked for it."

"I guess it's just luck that Willie Uptegrove sends off $500 to the Congressman every year," Leo said. "Don't you deny it, Rosie Uptegrove. Dolores clears Willie's checks at the bank. Ain't that the truth, Dolores." Dolores ducked her head.

They argued the bridge rebuilding. Martha interrupted Leo whenever he moved to speak, and kept her mother Pickett supplied with cups of Nehi Orange. Over Big Rosie's shoulder Miracle saw Bradford Uptegrove work a pint from his pocket and tip its contents into a cup.

Bernie wondered if the rebuilding would reroute the highway away from the Miracle Inn. Big Rosie scoffed. "That

46

road will stay exactly where it is," she said. "There's no reason for it to change. You'll be making money hand over fist, Bernie Miracle. All those construction workers and contractors and government people will be coming through and the Miracle Inn is just the natural place for them to stop." She gave Rosamund a long wink. "That's not the only place they'll stop either, if I've got anything to say about it."

"Mamma!" Rosamund said. Her cheeks bloomed red and she tossed her black hair so that it brushed across Miracle's face. Miracle's heart rose to his throat. He uncrossed his legs and rearranged himself inside his pants.

"That's a fact now, Rosamund, you're twenty years old and old enough to be thinking about your future," Big Rosie said. "And if you don't I'll do some thinking for you. Your father knows every one of those contractors and they're not a bad bunch to know, either. Every one of them Yankees and half of them looking for the kind of woman you can't find in the big city. They'll be flocking here like ducks on a June bug. I wouldn't be surprised to see one show up a little early." A grin started at the corners of her eyes and worked its secret way to the corners of her mouth. "It wouldn't surprise me, not one bit. The early bird gets the worm."

"I thought you said Willie didn't know a soul," Leo said.

"Leo Miracle I'll thank you to keep your backbiting gossip to yourself," Big Rosie said. "Everybody knows you cut timber on Fort Knox land."

Across dinner Miracle drank a great deal and ate very little. Martha moved next to Big Rosie to discuss children and lumbago and to distract her from Leo. Miracle had no polite choice but to scoot away from Rosamund. He picked at his greens and thought what a fool he'd been to fall in love with a woman almost two years older than he, from across the river, whose father knew a U. S. Congressman and every rich single good-looking contractor to boot.

Every few minutes Rosamund directed a remark at him and offered him dishes. When Big Rosie wasn't looking, she sipped his beer. Her attentions only confused Miracle. His jaw sagged and when the others spoke to him he answered in grunts.

"Hey, hound dog," Bernie said. "Cheer up. You're why we're here." He reached across the table to slap his son's shoulder. "Have another beer," he said. He nodded at Martha's mother Pickett. "Have old Carrie Nation get it for you."

Miracle went to the beer tub. Rosamund followed. "Pour me a beer," she said.

"Your mother'll see," Miracle said.

"I'm twenty years old and I'll drink beer if I want," Rosamund said. "In a cup. No head."

They walked to the riffle, where the splash of water over the rocks and around the bridge pilings drowned the voices from the table. Miracle flopped on his back, tilting his head to the sky. "Why me Lord," he said, mournful as the whistle of the coal train that rumbled through at midnight.

Rosamund sat and sipped her beer. "I know just what you mean. All I want is to sing my way out of this hole and get to Nashville. I met this girl who's come to set things up for the Jamboree contest at the county fair—she works with one of those agencies—and she said anytime, honey, she said it just like that, anytime, honey, I'll get you in to see Mr. Porter Wagoner himself!"

"So you're clearing out."

"Isn't everybody? Ever since he got that job with the bridge contractor all you can get out of Bradford Uptegrove is California this, California that. 'When I get finished with this bridge job I'll have enough money to go to California,' he says. 'I'll buy me a car and move to Hollywood, where the money is easy and the women are too!' It's all part of his *plan*. I'm supposed to get married to some contractor he and Mamma have handpicked so I'm taken care of and he can take off to sit in the sun on the beach. Leaving me with screaming kids and dirty diapers and daytime TV. No sir,'' she said. ''No soap operas for me. The Grand Ol' Opry, maybe.''

Miracle eyed her sideways. ''So you're not getting married.''

''I'll marry whatever whenever I want, so long as it's headed to Nashville and has enough money to take me along,'' Rosamund said.

''And I'll push beer at the Miracle Inn.''

''You don't have to stay at the Inn any more than I have to get married to a Yankee contractor. You could go to California if you wanted. You can do anything. You're a man.''

''I can't leave. I could never leave. I'm a Miracle,'' he said. ''I'm *the* Miracle. Half the family doesn't even know my first name, and wouldn't use it if they did. I'll bet *you* don't know my first name.''

Rosamund stood. ''It's fine with me if you sit around this town feeling sorry for yourself. But you mark my word. The day will come when you'll see Rosamund Uptegrove up in lights.'' She walked to the river.

Miracle closed his eyes and thought about the songs his Grandma Miracle sang, about people who drowned themselves or stabbed themselves or hung themselves from high oak beams because they could not win their loves. He saw no future in that.

At the same time he saw no future in the Miracle Inn. With his father's stubbornness, Miracle knew that he would not give Rosamund up until she loved him or she loved somebody else.

Rosamund was right, after all. He was a man, this was

1967, people he knew were taking off for foreign places right and left. People who had grown up in Jessup County lived in Louisville and Cincinnati and Detroit. People Miracle knew were writing letters to their families from boot camp in South Carolina, even from Vietnam.

Two months ago a soldier from a town two counties over had been killed in a booby trap set by some Viet Cong, right in his home base, before he ever fired a gun. His picture had been in the *Argus*, and though nobody knew him several veterans of other wars went to the funeral and returned to give loud angry speeches in the Inn.

Things were happening out there, in California and Nashville and Vietnam, and he was nineteen and sitting on his butt in a field that smelled of cowpies.

"Rosamund! Ros-a-mund!" Big Rosie was yelling in a voice as sweet as sorghum. Rosamund ran to the table. Miracle rolled over to follow her with his eyes, across the slate bank to the sea of Miracles, gabbing and drinking and rowdy, with the Picketts scattered here and there, rocks of sobriety in the storm.

He lay studying this family, and the people that made him who he was and held him down, all at once: his mother Martha Pickett, her red hair filled with colors from the sun, without a wrinkle or spot or gray hair to show that she was a day older than the day she married; his father Bernie Miracle, whose hands darted from his beer to his elbows to his cigarette, and whose square jaw flushed bright red in the sun; the tables full of Miracles, all sharing some line of jaw or slump of shoulders or bow-legged walk that set them apart from the in-laws and friends and anybody else who was not family.

Then there were the Baptists from across the river, Big Rosie and Willie Uptegrove and their children: Bradford Uptegrove, who would never be happier, making plans with

50

money he'd yet to earn, dating quiet LaHoma Dean, who'd give him no trouble along the way; and Rosamund, her back to Miracle but her black hair spread across shoulders as white and wonderful and cold as January snow.

And the others, all talking with one eye cocked at a stranger wearing a wide paisley tie with a coat to match. He had blond hair—nobody in Jessup County had blond hair, or wore a tie, except to funerals or weddings. He was not older but getting there, not fat but thick enough to be prosperous. He shook women's hands—Miracle saw him take his mother's hand. He pecked his mother's cheek, as if he'd known her since Adam. This, Miracle figured, must be Big Rosie's Yankee contractor.

*   *   *

Martha saw him first. Across babies and wicker baskets and crabgrass she saw the bright red car, with a blond man different from Bernie in every way: thick where Bernie was thin, pale where Bernie was raw red, soft where Bernie was hard. In the bright May light there was no mistaking this Yankee's hair, yellow as goldenrod. He climbed from the car and caught her staring. She blushed and looked back to her food. A minute later she stole a glance up. He was still looking at her, his eyes staring coolly across Big Rosie's welcoming bulk.

He stepped through swarming babies, and held out his hand to her, before all others. "Talbott Marquand," he said. He squeezed her hand, a second longer and a little tighter than he ought? Or was that her imagination? Or was that her hope? Before she could loosen her grasp, he drew her cheek to his lips and planted a kiss, bold and firm. She was too shocked to resist.

She rose abruptly. "Pleased to meet you," she said coldly. "Got to tend to the kids."

Across the next hour she felt his eyes on her back. She

51

turned around once or twice, quickly, to find him engaged in a perfectly normal conversation, with the glazed smile of someone bored to tears but too polite to say as much. She cursed her imagination and turned back, only to feel his eyes again, checking her out in a way she'd not felt in twenty-three years, since leaving the Miracle Inn that first time, under Bernie's watchful stare.

She was stern with herself. She kept her attention on the children, the table, the women, all the while she felt that the churning in her stomach must be giving her away. When Big Rosie cornered the newcomer and Rosamund, Martha breathed a sigh of relief. She was too old, and too married, for this nonsense.

But across the afternoon her thoughts returned to his first cool stare, with the sun glinting from his yellow, yellow hair.

*   *   *

The sycamore shadows crept across the river and the water flowed the color of blackstrap molasses. Miracle gathered himself up one long limb at a time and loped across the field.

At the side tables the Miracles were putting away beer bottles and leftovers and babies. At the center table Martha was changing the diaper on a niece, the squirming baby neatly spreadeagled on a towel. Big Rosie Uptegrove and Leo Miracle were glaring at each other with withering eyes. Leo was shouting and pointing at the ground. "Our country!" he said. "This is our country, right here, and every damned one of them boys should be over there defending it."

"Over there is not over here, Leo Miracle, and I'll be damned if I can see how giving up our guns and our boys to a bunch of slant-eyed foreigners is going to protect our country," Big Rosie said.

"It's the Chinese," Bernie said.

"I hears thunder," Ossetta said, looking up at the cloudless sky.

"It's the guns at Fort Knox," Leo said, as if she were a fool indeed. He turned to Bernie. "It was a different country in World War II and that didn't stop us from going over."

"And where were you in World War II?" Big Rosie said. "As if I didn't know."

"The country needed me to farm," Leo said. "I volunteered but they wouldn't take me."

"And the country needs Bradford Uptegrove to rebuild the Boatyard Bridge."

"Which don't need rebuilding in the first place."

"It's the Chinese, the Chinese are behind all this," Bernie said.

"I smells rain," Ossetta said. "*That* ain't Fort Knox." She began gathering dishes. The Yankee contractor stood shifting his weight from one leg to another and looking into the dark trees as if something interesting might be found there.

"The Chinese started the whole thing to get us fighting amongst ourselves," Bernie said. "Then when our backs are turned, they're going to march in and take over."

"Bernie Miracle, you stay out of this," Martha said. She skewered the diaper with a practiced thrust. "This is a graduation party, not the Miracle Inn." She bounced the baby and waggled a finger into its smooth pale face before turning it over to a hovering sister-in-law. "Why people can't get together for a reunion without acting like they have to solve the problems of the world that haven't ever been solved and never will be solved—well, it's beyond me."

"Now *that* woman's talking sense," the Yankee contractor said.

Martha started and blushed. No one spoke, as if the contractor's words reminded them that there was an outsider here, a

Yankee, who might leave with the impression that these Southerners disagreed about important matters.

Leo rushed to fill the gap. "She's been watching too much TV," he said. "I *told* Bernie when he moved that thing into his house, I said you watch what happens, a woman at home all day with nothing to do but sit in front of that tube—but he wouldn't listen, no sir, not to little brother. You'll never see Dolores with one of them things, I guarantee that. 'The starved hen clucks loudest,' 'swhat I always say."

Big Rosie stood and grabbed her pocketbook. "I refuse to listen to any more of this manure," she said. "Bradford Uptegrove, you take us home. Rosamund, you ride with Mr. Marquand. I don't believe he's quite familiar with the way."

Miracle moved next to Rosamund as she gathered dishes from the table. "Meet me tonight under the bridge," he said. It rolled from his tongue like grace before supper.

Rosamund didn't blink but sat down, careful as a waitress carrying two plates on either arm. "What for," she said.

"Just to talk. We could talk about going away, getting out."

"And what makes you think I'd be interested in going with you?"

"Not with me. I told you, *I* can't leave. But we could talk about it, where *you'd* go."

"And where is that?"

Miracle shrugged. "Meet me at the bridge. We'll figure it out together."

She stood. "Sorry, Miracle, I'd be a liar if I said I'd make it. Not with Mamma forcefeeding me to Mr. Marquand."

"When can I see you again, then."

"Come to the county fair Jamboree contest. Watch me sing. Cheer me on." She smiled past him, so big and bright that Miracle turned around.

54

Bradford Uptegrove was herding the stranger in their direction. "This is the man I told you about, Miracle," Bradford said. "This is the man that showed me the light. I'd still be shoveling shit except for this man's advice." He grabbed up the stranger's hand. "Mr. Marquand, Mr. Talbott Marquand, there's one person you haven't met, the guest of honor. Miracle, meet Mr. Talbott Marquand, my future boss and builder of the new bridge. Miracle here, he runs the Miracle Inn with his father, the tavern you saw just the other side of the bridge."

"You've got yourself quite a spot there," Talbott said. "That must turn a nice profit."

"We get by," Miracle said.

"Getting by is one thing. Getting rich is another," Talbott said. "You and your father want to do something with that spot, you let me know. You could tear that shack down, put in a hamburger stand with a liquor license. Make a fortune. You're sitting on a gold mine and you haven't even sunk a pick." He shook Miracle's hand. "Talbott Marquand," he said. He gave Miracle a card, then took Rosamund's hand and led her to his car, a scarlet Mustang with bucket seats and a convertible top.

"You see?" Bradford said. "That man has got the ways and the means to get you somewhere. You should've been more friendly, Miracle."

Miracle watched as Talbott lowered the top. He helped Rosamund into her seat and drove away. When they reached the levee he turned north, towards New Hope and the Miracle Inn.

"He'll be back, Miracle," Bradford said. "If there's money to be made or women to be had he'll be back, and there's both here. Next time be more friendly. You got to hustle people like him if you're going to get anywhere in the world."

55

The Mustang crossed the Boatyard Bridge. Planks rumbled, girders creaked. Hands in his pockets, Miracle watched Rosamund sail through the girders and cables, her black hair streaming in the wind.

Behind Miracle's back, Martha watched, too, but her eyes were not on Rosamund Uptegrove. Through the first drops of Ossetta's thunderstorm she followed Talbott Marquand, soft and thick, with his Yankee voice and his Yankee manners and his blond, blond hair.

CHAPTER III

Something Changed

AFTER GRADUATION, Miracle started morning shifts at the Miracle Inn. Each day he rose at six to open the Inn for the men who bought beer for the two-hour drive to their jobs in chemical plants or distilleries in Louisville. All day he worked at the same chores that his father and grandfather had done before him and that (if Bernie had his way) Miracle's sons and grandsons would do after he was dead.

Miracle was working day shift when Talbott Marquand brought his bulldozers to begin the latest version of the Boatyard Bridge. From the Inn door Miracle watched the parade of machines. Everyone in town lined the street and pointed and nodded his head. It was like a circus come to a town that had never seen a circus. Miracle watched, wide-eyed as the rest, wearing a white apron and holding a broom, until Talbott drove by in a tractor trailer as long as the Inn, pulling a canary yellow bulldozer with Bradford Uptegrove atop it and a gleaming silver construction helmet atop Bradford. Miracle ran inside, to toss his apron and broom behind the bar.

With construction underway, life changed around the Inn. New noises drowned the old morning routine. By the time Miracle reached the Inn, bulldozers were scraping great orange scars across the bottomland. Clay dust was thick in the air, except when it rained; then the dust settled in a soft, sticky veneer on the bottles behind the Inn's bar. In the mornings the construction workers lined up at the Inn behind the commuters to the Louisville factories. Miracle was too frantic for conversation with the regulars, who grumbled about the poor service.

Talbott came every day for lunch. He stood alone at the end of the colored bar, in clothes that looked as if they were taking a rest from Ossetta's steam iron instead of having been at work building a bridge. He drank one Michelob and ate a single pickled sausage with saltines from the big glass jars at either end of the bar. Once a week he told Bernie how he should hire Marquand's firm to tear down the Inn, pave the parking lot, and build a carryout restaurant with a liquor license.

At five Bernie's brother Leo came to take the evening shift. Miracle walked to the Boatyard Bridge, to watch the construction from under the north pilings. He could get liquor from the Inn storeroom but he kept a store of beer in a cool concrete crevice in the bridge pilings. At the end of these long days he sat drinking and watching the construction crew fold up for the day.

Miracle had been making trips to the north pilings of the Boatyard Bridge since long before that summer. In high school he climbed down to the pilings to drink from his private stash of beer. He took a transistor radio and tuned in WLS, beaming across the plains (flat land!) between Kentucky and Chicago. He heard songs he didn't understand, sung by a generation he was supposed to be part of, songs about drugs and sex and the

58

sins of the flag. With WLS in one hand and a beer in the other, Miracle pondered the problems of his life.

The beer and the melancholy rumble of the planks under the car wheels made Miracle feel sorry for himself for being alone and in high school and wanting to see the world and wanting sex. Usually he ended the evening by smashing his bottles against the north pilings and masturbating into the river. This gave him a great sense of relief. Across those years the brown glass surrounding the north pilings grew steadily higher.

Miracle had just smashed an evening's bottles and was relieving his other tensions, that night he first met Bradford and Rosamund Uptegrove.

Bradford had been setting bankpoles when he heard the bottles smashing. He suspected a group of Fort Knox soldiers, who drove from the base to buy liquor but had nowhere to go but New Hope to drink it. He explored with his flashlight. He caught Miracle pants down, working his pecker to beat the band.

It was not yet June and Miracle shone winter white in the flashlight's glare. He had Bernie's square jaw and Bernie's angular joints, with Martha's hair the color of broken brick and eyes like chipped robin's eggs. With his hair standing up and his bare knobby knees he looked like a poor relation to the great tufted herons that waded the river on long skinny legs.

"What are you doing here," Bradford asked.

Miracle considered. "Swimming?"

"Think again," Bradford said. He was a thick, squat man, a head shorter and six years older than Miracle, with big arms and a barrel chest covered with hair that continued up his neck to become the black dots that covered his chin.

Bradford turned around to find Rosamund had crept up behind him. She knew Miracle by reputation and was absorbing his nakedness with as much interest as Martha had surveyed the Miracle Inn on her first visit, years before. "Get back to the car, Sister," Bradford said. She backed a few steps away.

Bradford thought his sister ought to be embarrassed and that he ought to take steps to avenge the embarrassment she ought to feel. On the other hand, he recognized Miracle's face from the Inn, and had known of him since his birth. Bradford solved this dilemma by tossing Miracle in the river, then helping him out.

He handed Miracle a set of bankpoles. Miracle helped them finish setting their poles, though he baited the hooks so the bait would fall off. Mostly he kept his eyes on Rosamund.

When Bradford struggled down the bank to tie up a line, Miracle, true to his mother's blood, seized his chance. "So you're Rosamund Uptegrove," he said.

"That's right."

"I know you. You sing. You sang last winter at the high school."

Rosamund smiled slightly, as if she were pleased in spite of herself to be known. "You're right. I recommend you remember it."

"And why should I remember it," Miracle said, though he had no intention of forgetting.

"Because I'm going to be a star," she said, as simple and positive as cornbread.

"O-oh. On television? Or in Hollywood?" The smallest derision crept into his voice.

She ignored his tone. "I'm starting in Nashville. That's where my voice and my interests lead me. It's easier to get established there. Then maybe I'll move on. Depends on the offers."

"People don't go from Nashville to Hollywood."

"People *you* know, maybe. Those people don't include *me*."

60

Overhead the canopy of water maples and sycamores was alive with the grind and chatter of katydids and locusts. Miracle and Rosamund were surrounded by lightning bugs, their numbers doubled in the river's glossy black mirror. Miracle wanted to reach out and touch her shoulder, so badly the tips of his fingers tingled. He considered. He wasn't likely to see her again, not soon; she had her side of the river, he had his. He worked his hand along a branch behind her back.

"We'd better help Bradford," she said, "else he'll not catch a single fish, I know him. Then he'll blame it on me, just like he always does."

They finished by midnight. Bradford told Miracle to meet him in the morning to check the lines. When they parted in the light of the waning moon Miracle could have sworn that behind her brother's back, Rosamund winked.

After that night Miracle and Bradford hunted and fished and trapped together. Miracle kept an eye out for Rosamund, but Bradford never brought her along. Through the driveup window of the Inn, Miracle saw her many times, always in a crowd of men who looked old enough to know better. If she remembered the boy who handed her the beer through the window, she gave no sign of it. But for Miracle the memory of her wide eyes that evening when she caught him breaking bottles haunted the north pilings. He never returned there without seeing her face and conjecturing her body. From across the river Miracle decided he was in love.

He had pursued her ever since, with the persistence and luck of a greenhorn on a snipe hunt. Working at the Miracle Inn, shoving beer through the driveup window to Baptist tobacco farmers, Miracle considered how much his pursuit of Rosamund Uptegrove was exactly like hunting snipe: the closer he thought he'd got, the farther away she was.

61

* * *

The summer after Miracle's graduation wound down, to the opening of the county fair. Miracle worked late night shifts at the Inn, so he could be certain to be free for Rosamund's appearance in Saturday night's Jamboree contest.

On Saturday afternoon of the fair, business was slow. In the river bottoms the idle bulldozers and backhoes shimmered in waves of heat. Across the river Miracle could hear the grind and chatter of the ferris wheel.

The Inn was dim but it held the August heat as nicely as any oven. Bernie thought this a good idea, as it made people drink more beer. He was drinking a beer now, rolling the sweating bottle across his flushed forehead and cheeks between sips.

"I hope you're planning to work tonight," Bernie said to Miracle.

Miracle watched the yellow stripe that wandered over the Jackson Highway before petering out at the one-lane levee. "As a matter of fact, I wasn't," he said, not looking at Bernie.

"It's going to be a big night. You know that. Leo can't work. He's got two horses to show. I can't work. I'm judging the barrel races. You know all that. I told you that a month ago."

Miracle had known that but in all his planning he had pushed the knowledge to the back of his mind. He had no one to blame but himself.

"You got to get used to that, " Bernie said. "You're responsible for a business. People depend on you. People find out they can't depend on you, they don't come, they go someplace else. The Inn has been here longer than any place else in town because people know they can depend on me. And I give it over to you because I know I can depend on you.

62

There's nobody else I feel comfortable about turning this place over to alone, not even Leo.''

"The Inn has been here longer than any place else because it's the first goddamn place across the bridge," Miracle growled.

Bernie shrugged. "Maybe so. But that don't change the situation. We got to have somebody here tonight. You're the only one free. There'll be other fairs. Take a extra day off next week. But when the business is there you got to meet it."

Bernie left. For a half hour business was brisk, then everyone left for the fair. Miracle stepped out back and sat watching the sunset across the river bottoms. To the west the flare of the Fort Knox guns lit the underside of the clouds with brilliant flashes. To the south Miracle could make out the topmost car of the ferris wheel as it circled above the clumps of sycamores lining the river.

The front door banged. Miracle cursed his luck, then resigned himself to an evening at the Inn.

It was Martha, dressed in a sleeveless scarlet dress with thin arm straps. Miracle had never seen her dressed so. She looked as if in daylight she would be positively shocking.

"I've come to take your place," she said, leaning over the bar.

"I thought you and Father were going to the fair together."

"I met him at home. He told me you were down here. *Stuck* down here. I sent him on his way, told him I'd be over later."

With her foot propped on the brass rail and a beer in one hand, she looked alarmingly pretty for a mother, anybody's mother, let alone Miracle's own. Where Bernie's hands never rested, hers stayed wrapped around her beer as if she expected it at any moment to fly from her grasp. While she sipped and talked she twisted in a slow circle, taking in every corner and

63

shelf of the Inn, as if comparing it to other places she knew, or deciding how it might better be arranged. When she had turned in a complete circle she turned her eyes to him. "Stop that," she said.

"Stop what?"

"Picking at your shirt. Bernie does that. Drives me wild."

"Oh." Miracle dangled his hands at his sides. He searched for something to say. "So why did you come down here, if you knew he was coming home?"

"I told you. I came to take your place. And I wanted to catch you here. I wanted to talk to you here." She looked about, another slow circle. "I came down here because I want to do what I can to keep this place from getting in your blood. I can't stop you from working here and I don't want to. It's a pretty rough crowd you're traveling with here but I guess you know that. You can make some money and get some experience. But I want you to get out in the world before you settle down here. See some places I never saw. Go to college, next year, or the year after, if that's what you want. I want you to promise me you'll do that. Get out and see the world, anyway, before you settle into running the Miracle Inn."

"I'll promise that," Miracle said, remembering his conversation with Rosamund at his graduation picnic. Maybe I'll go to Nashville, he thought. Maybe I'll go with Rosamund.

At the driveup window the buzzer sounded. The customer ordered two fifths of Wild Turkey and a bottle of Asti Spumanti. Miracle could not see the faces in the dark of the car, but in all of Jessup County only Rosamund drank Asti Spumanti and only Talbott talked with a Yankee accent. And Rosamund was driving; lacquered nails reached for the change. Then they were gone, the brand new Mustang with a little Knobs Fork mud on the wheels screeching around the Inn amd throwing gravel against the windows. Through the front window Miracle watched the Mustang taillights disappear onto the levee.

This bar was as familiar to him as home, and he saw without seeing the pool table you played to the north, and the big windows, and the beveled mirror fronted with bottles, and the U of a bar that he thought of as a stock pen with himself as the penned steer, waiting dumbly for slaughter: half pale oak and half dark mahogany, this pen, and carved into the oak bar the sun that changed from rising to setting depending on how many beers you'd had. Only Martha made the scene any different from any slow night, in her scarlet dress like gashed flesh against the dark wooden bar.

She nodded at the window. "It's a good thing whoever that was didn't come inside or I'd probably have cost us another customer."

"He doesn't know about such things."

"Who's that?"

"Talbott Marquand. With Rosamund Uptegrove at the wheel."

"Oh. Oh-h-h. So that was Talbott."

"Who else orders Wild Turkey. And Asti Spumanti. In this whole county Rosamund Uptegrove is the only person I know who drinks Asti Spumanti. I don't like that man," Miracle said. It was out before he thought about it.

Martha raised her eyes from her beer. "Oh? Why not?"

"I don't know. His Yankee ways, I guess." Miracle's real reasons had to do with Rosamund, but he thought better of mentioning that. "Coming in here. Bossing everybody around. Acting like he owns the town, even this place. You know he talks about tearing this place down? Wants to put in a Dairy Freeze. Hunh."

"So let him talk. Talk never killed a Thanksgiving turkey."

Miracle frowned. Here was his girlfriend dating Talbott Marquand, and his mother taking up for the guy.

Martha drained her beer and set it on the bar. She ducked under the flap. "On the other side," she said. Miracle balked, unable to decide whether his mother was drunk or simply making a fool of him. "Come on, I need some practice running this place. Get over there and order something."

Miracle ducked under the bar. Martha took up the towel. "I'll have a fifth of your cheapest whisky, to go," Miracle said.

"I can't wait on you there. That's the colored bar."

Miracle snorted. "Since when have there been enough coloreds in New Hope to set aside a whole bar? All that stopped ages ago."

"So Bernie does change some things around here," Martha said. "I'll be damned."

"I don't know that he had much to do with it," Miracle said. "More like recognizing the facts. Ever since Ossetta's kids moved to Lexington there's hardly any coloreds left to drink, and the ones left have figured out better places to do it. Can't say as I blame them there, if you want my opinion."

Martha bundled the liquor with clumsy hands. "You're using the wrong size sack," Miracle said.

"Miracle. Please." She laid the sack on the counter. "On the house. Now get out of here and get over to the fair and have a good time. If you make it snappy you can catch the Jamboree contest. Don't let Bernie see you whatever you do. He'll find out anyway but I'd just as soon tell him on my own sweet time."

"What about closing? What about the register?"

"You ask too damn many questions," Martha said.

66

"Whose son are you anyway. Get going before I change my mind. And don't forget your bourbon."

He was outside before he stopped to think. Through the front window he saw her lean her elbows on the bar, watching, wearing the dress she must have put on for this occasion, a bright red blossom in the dim light.

On the bridge he pulled the bourbon from the sack. There were two bottles, the second double-wrapped and tucked beside the first. He pulled the sack from the second bottle. Next to a fifth of Wild Turkey was a bottle of Asti Spumanti.

*   *   *

At the fair Miracle climbed to the farthest, darkest corner of the grandstand, just as Rosamund was accepting her award. The outcome had never been in doubt. She had written her own songs and music, she had the best voice in the county, she was the daughter of Willie Uptegrove, who sat on the County Fair Central Committee.

She wore blue, a floor-length royal blue gown of some filmy material, cut low in front and back, with a bodice of blue sequins. In the glare of the track lights she looked pale, but the rose in her cheeks stood out and with her black hair flowing across her breast and her pale skin blushing she looked like Barbara Allen come to life.

A cascade of roses with legs sticking out walked around one end of the grandstand. Miracle could not see the person behind the flowers, but very few men in Jessup County could afford that many roses and only one would spend that kind of money on flowers.

They were all together on the stage, Willie and Big Rosie and Rosamund and Talbott Marquand, looking more like a family portrait than Miracle liked to think. The Jamboree band

67

took the stage behind them. Rosamund sang "Fox on the Run" and "My Elusive Dreams" and finished with "The Great Speckled Bird," drawing coughs and catcalls from the Catholic side of the bleachers. Then she asked her friends to visit her at the backstage trailer and she stepped down, elegant and measured as the queen of England, her right hand lifting billows of blue chiffon, her left hand in Talbott Marquand's.

Following Rosamund, Miracle lost himself in the crowd. Outside the backstage trailer he stood behind a pile of rabbit hutches from the 4-H. He tucked the Asti Spumanti under a bale of hay. Feeling like a lowland Democrat in a crowd of mountain Republicans, Miracle moved forward. He decided he would leave all moves to Rosamund. If she ignored him, he would retire to the bridge pilings and cry into his whiskey until time to meet Martha at the Inn.

Rosamund saw him through the crowd. She lifted Talbott's arm from hers and crossed the sawdust. She threw her arms around him and kissed his cheek. She seized his hand. "I'm going!" she cried. "I'm on my way! You *have* to visit me. Give me your promise."

Miracle was blinded by sequins and love. She was beautiful, exotic, famous, as different from New Hope and the Miracle Inn as Catholic from Baptist, North from South, sweet sin from dull virtue. "You let me know when you're going to be there, and how long," he said. "I'll come."

"I'll be there 'til hell freezes over." She shook his hand loose. "I'm going places, Miracle, if you hadn't figured that out by now you're slower than I thought. You talk to Talbott. He's been to the Grand Ol' Opry more times than you've crossed the bridge and he says I did as well as anybody he's seen there." She lowered her voice. "He's promised to help me out once I get there." She flounced her dress. "I told you

you'd see me up in lights. You will." She craned her neck, long and white. Her breasts surged against the blue sequins. "I wonder where Talbott went. He was right over by the roses."

But Miracle had not heard. His eyes were stuck on Bernie, approaching across the sawdust with the grim steadiness of a Fort Knox tank.

* * *

In the Inn a Budweiser clock hung above the bar, with ducks flapping eternally across a mountain waterfall. Martha endured the steady slap of the duck wings for longer than she thought possible before searching for the plug. She was crouched behind the bar, searching, when she heard the door open. She scrambled to her feet.

It was Talbott Marquand. Surprised, Martha met his eyes. She kept his glance a moment longer than she ought; then a moment longer still.

He did not give her the chance to look away. "The Uptegrove party is celebrating. A rising star on the southern horizon," he said. "They sent me to replenish the cooler."

"No need to order. I know what they drink." Martha bagged vodka for Big Rosie and a soft drink for Willie. She set the sack on the bar with a hard thump. "Anything else?"

His eyes held hers. "I'll have a beer," he said. "Something local." She pulled an Oertel's from the cooler and set it on the bar, avoiding his eyes. "So," he said. "Why is a beautiful woman like you shoving beer across a bartop in the backwoods of Kentucky?"

Oldest trick in the book, Martha thought. Ten answers putting him in his place sprang to her lips. She said none of them. A rise out of her—that was what he wanted. She thought of Bernie, and the twenty-three years since the last compliment she'd heard from a man. She fixed Talbott with a hard glare, empty of flirtation. "Because of love," she said. "You want a glass?"

He flinched. Bernie, or any other man Martha knew, would never have flinched. Martha felt a wave of remorse. She set a glass on the bar, opened and poured his beer. In her answer she heard those years with Bernie, without love. Was that this man's fault? Her heart resisted the question with the stubbornness she'd learned from Bernie. *She'd* not be caught making the first move. She said nothing.

Talbott took up his beer. "I guess I should have known before I asked," he said. The joking was gone from his voice. "It's the only possible answer, when you think about it."

"I try not to."

"I'm here to tell you that doesn't work. But I guess you know that. The real question is, why did you tell me? I've been down here almost three months and that's the first straight answer I've got from a soul."

"Straight," Martha said with a grimace. "What is *straight*."

"The truth. Told straight on. No devious sidetracks. No obscene references to racial heritage. No grand embellishments."

"You're looking for that? *Here*?"

Talbott pointed his beer glass at her. "*You* told the truth."

"I have a reputation for that." In the dim bar light his blond hair stood out like a patch of frost against the dark. Martha felt stirring in her the queasiness of the day of Miracle's graduation, when she first met this blond Yankee.

He gave her no time to rest, or think, or retreat to the storeroom. "Then life with Bernie Miracle is all that bad," he said.

"No," Martha said. She pressed her thumbnail into her

70

beer label, tearing it free in crumpled strips. She should tell a man anything, because he was fast and free with his compliments? Certainly not. Yet she felt heavy as sin the need to tell someone something, her side of the story. "It's way more complicated than that," she said.

"So? I got the time."

She smiled, shaking her head. "Sorry. Twenty years you ain't got."

He reached across her beer to touch her fingertips. "Neither do you."

She pulled her hand away, but she told him her story then. She took a cigarette from his pack, the first she'd smoked in years. After one puff she left it sitting, its smoke curling around the nape of her neck.

She told him how she'd grown up Baptist, how she'd crossed the river on a dare, how she'd fought with Bernie, how everything had been so different from what she had hoped.

He laid his hand across hers, too firm for her to slip it away. "So why did you marry him?"

"Love," she said, not quick and hard, as she'd said it earlier, but slow and thoughtful. "I married Bernie Miracle because I thought things would be different, and better, across the river. I came into a Catholic church, Assumption Church, and it was so full of mystery, after my life. I smelled the incense and saw the candles, and that was so new, and different. And it was so positive, so certain what was right and what was wrong. Bernie was part of that. He lived across the river, he was Catholic. I was tired of being comfortable, I wanted to stir up the bucket, I saw and met a man I could do that with. I thought. All that, and love. I just plain fell in love."

"With all the wrong reasons for falling in love."

"Then you must know the right reasons. Tell me, please." He said nothing. She sighed and drew her hand from his.

71

"Bernie Miracle is a good man. I've got as good a marriage as there is in this town, or so my friends tell me, and I believe them. Bernie provides well, I can usually depend on him to be where he says he'll be, give or take an hour or so, he goes to church, even if he falls asleep once he's there. Me, I've stayed away from drink, which is more than most women I know. I've stayed away from Fort Knox soldiers. I was young and rambunctious and I did something stupid, maybe, but less stupid than what a lot of women have done. And at least I've learned—you haven't seen me trying it again, and you won't, either. I do my share of staring out the window, but there's a lot of that around here."

She turned to the register, pretending to count cash. She wondered why she had opened her heart to Talbott Marquand, a Yankee with whom she'd shared a friendly beer at the Miracle Inn.

She would like to believe that earlier that evening she had chosen this dress because it was festive, and in New Hope she had so few chances to be festive. It wasn't every night she tended bar at the Miracle Inn. She would like to believe she was here only to give her son a chance to get Rosamund Uptegrove out of his system. Unless that happened there was no moving on for him, and only by spending time with her would he get her out of his system. Experience taught her that.

All this she would like to believe, and no more. All this was true, Talbott would call it the truth, and once, years before, she could have believed it and stopped there. But she knew herself too well now to ignore what stirred beyond and behind Talbott's truth. After twenty years the time and the place were right. She was wanting something, some change, as restless as the birds that soared aimlessly above lush August fields, their chicks raised and nothing to do but wait for winter's coming. Her restlessness had no name that she could put in words but it

72

stirred her heart as surely as years before it had driven her across the river.

She turned to the mirror and caught a glimpse of herself between bottles of whiskey and sloe gin. A married woman, a mother, forty-five years old, in a scarlet dress resurrected from the attic. She thought of her first mistake so long before, crossing the river to marry a man for all the wrong reasons. Never again, she thought. Never a fool for love.

"So now it's my turn," Talbott said. "Why I came to New Hope. Why I came to the Miracle Inn." He started, stopped, studied the floor. "I came because of love. Or lack of it, I guess. If you're interested."

"I'm not," Martha said. She faced him, square and cold again. "You want another beer, you got to pay for the first."

"Yes, *sir*." Talbott laid a dollar on the bar. "Two more. On me." Martha shrugged and bent to the cooler. It had been long enough since anyone had bought her a drink or anything else. She would allow him this much. No more.

Then the front door slammed and she lifted her eyes. Across the bar, she met Bernie's stare, cold and hard as broken glass.

* * *

Outside in the Inn parking lot, Miracle read the Budweiser clock through the window. It was eleven-thirty. Inside, Talbott Marquand stood with his back to the door. Miracle saw no sign of Martha.

At the fair Bernie had been bright red, the veins on his nose standing out in mapped relief. When Miracle told him Martha was tending bar Bernie had turned gray. He'd sat heavily on the trailer step, holding his head in his hands. Miracle was on the verge of asking if he needed help when Bernie raised his head and walked to the car.

Bernie was waiting at the screen door now. When Miracle

reached the door Bernie let it fall to, in Miracle's face. Miracle caught the door and eased it shut behind him. He turned around.

Martha emerged from under the bar. Talbott raised his beer to Bernie from across the room, flashing a wide grin. "How about one, Bernie? On me."

Bernie did not raise his voice, though Miracle heard ground glass under his words. "It's closing time. I came to close."

Martha set two beers before Talbott. "Closing can wait," she said, without so much as a quaver. "He just bought those beers."

"Get a third," Talbott said. "Four. One for the boy. We got to celebrate. We saw a star rise on the southern horizon." He was drunk. Miracle realized with a start that they were all drunk.

"I don't want a beer," Bernie said. "He don't want a beer."

"You might let the boy speak for himself."

"He's my son," Bernie said. "I can speak for him. It's closing time. The law says I got to be closed by midnight on Saturdays."

"That's the first time I've heard anything about law in this town," Talbott said.

"Finish your beer," Bernie said.

"Take your time," Martha said. She set two glasses on the bar, tilted a beer into one. She took a sip. "Tell me about the contest." She leaned on her elbows.

Miracle moved to stand beside the pool table. He felt as if he were walking through deep water, growing deeper every second, where each move took longer than it ought.

Bernie ducked under the bar flap. His hands fluttered in constant motion along the bar, searching along independent of his vision or thoughts until they located a small object, a salt shaker or an ashtray or one of the crisp white slices of raw potato that the Catholics liked to eat with their beer. He picked it up, whatever object he'd found, and pored over it with his hands, turning it this way and that like a squirrel with a nut, until his hands were satisfied and he moved on to the next object in reach. When he got to the end of the bar he stood silent, playing with his shirt sleeves, folding and unfolding his cuffs and picking at his elbows.

"I guess I should be going," Talbott said.

"Take your time," Martha said.

"I guess I'll go," Talbott said. "I told those folks I'd be back in ten minutes." Bernie said nothing. Talbott picked up his sack and spilled some change onto the bar. The quarters jingled. One fell to the floor. Martha bent to pick it up. "See you later," Talbott said. Martha stood. "Come back," she said. Talbott eased the door shut. "Anytime," she said.

Talbott's Mustang pulled quietly onto the levee and turned south. Martha picked up the beers and glasses. "So now I get to learn to close. I told you you didn't need to worry, Miracle."

"What the hell are you doing here," Bernie said.

The air thinned. Miracle caught his breath. "I called her," he said.

"You stay out of this," Bernie said.

"No," Miracle said. The eight ball was near a side pocket and he rolled it from one hand to the other across the green baize, keeping his eyes carefully on the ball. "I wanted to see the races. So I called her and asked her to come down for an hour or two. I got caught up in the contest and wanting to see Rosamund Uptegrove sing and I didn't get back."

"Sure you did," Martha said. "Here you are. High time, too. I was just about to close myself." She raised the flap in the bar.

Bernie caught her hand. "A married woman. My wife,

75

tending bar. In a dress like that.'' He reached across the bar to pluck at one of the scarlet spaghetti straps.

Martha drew back. ''I can't see how this dress is going to hurt business. That's what you're worried about, isn't it? Business?''

Bernie slammed the flap down. Miracle jumped. The eight ball rolled from his hand. ''You're trying to ruin this place,'' Bernie said. ''That's your plan. You close the place down and then there's nothing left to pass on and you can send that boy anywhere you want.''

''Bernie calm down,'' Martha said. Miracle retrieved the eight ball, keeping one eye on his mother.

In those few minutes with Bernie something changed. Suddenly things moved too fast instead of too slow. Martha lifted the bar flap and let it slam behind her, harder than Bernie had slammed it before. She strode towards the door, talking as she went. ''Five people came in tonight. Two were in town for the fair, I'd never seen them before. I told the others Miracle was sick and you had to judge and they thought nothing of it.'' She picked up her purse midstride, with a swoop of her hand. At the door she paused. ''You coming,'' she said to Miracle.

''Where to?''

''The fair,'' she said. ''I can still hear the ferris wheel.''

Miracle looked at Bernie quickly, then down at the pool table. He rolled the eight ball back and forth. ''I guess if you don't need me around here—'' Bernie turned to the beveled mirror. ''Rosamund is still waiting, and Bradford Uptegrove and Big Rosie and Willie—'' Bernie did not turn around. Miracle left the eight ball sitting. As he walked outside he heard it drop with a solid thunk into the north corner pocket.

Martha gunned the accelerator as Miracle climbed in. ''Let's take this thing to town!'' she cried gaily, and they were off. Miracle could not keep from glancing back at the Inn.

Bernie was rubbing up and down the mahogany, not looking out the window or at anything Miracle could tell. With no customers framing him he looked forlorn and out of place, as if he'd stumbled behind the bar by mistake and was trying, like a fly trapped behind a windowpane, to find his way out.

Then they were on the bridge, flying between girders. Halfway across Martha screeched to a halt. "You were good," she said. "Your mother's son. You got any of that Wild Turkey left?"

Miracle reached under the seat. Martha took a swig from the bottle. Miracle thought he should be shocked, though he was unsure exactly what he should be shocked at. Before tonight he had never realized how pretty his mother was, with smooth white hands and hair that glowed red even in the dim light from the dash.

She handed him the bottle. "Have a drink. Come on. I know you're not happy about leaving Bernie. I'm not happy about leaving him either. But if we're neither one happy about it, if we don't watch out we'll end up back there, sulking in an empty bar. And what's the point of *that*. So drink up. Did you get that Italian stuff to Rosamund Uptegrove?" Miracle shook his head. Martha wrinkled her forehead in annoyance. "I didn't put it there for nothing. I guess I'll just have to figure out a way to get you and her together. You pay attention, now, I'm not always going to be there to take care of your business. Take a drink," she said, not a request but a command. "We're about to get into trouble. We might as well toast the fact."

Car lights flickered at the south end of the bridge. Miracle swigged. Martha stepped on the gas. "She's not going to do you any good," she said.

"Sure she is. She already has."

"If you call being miserable doing you good, then you're in seventh heaven. But they told me that, twenty years ago. It'll take some doing to get her out of your system, and I'm not the one to do it.''

Miracle sat silent until they parked at the fairgrounds. He was too overwhelmed by his mother and the way she was talking, and by his own behavior, walking out on Bernie, to say a word. He liked her wildness and deep inside himself he felt a wild string vibrating in harmony. At the same time he wondered if he shouldn't save his mother from herself. In her mood God knew where she might take them both.

At the fairgrounds the bare bulbs swung forlornly in the trees and the air was thick with dust and the rich smell of manure. Trash skittered along the ground. Stray dogs humped in the bushes.

"You stay on your toes now," Martha said. "Be your mother's son. It becomes you." She put out her arm to stop him. "I'll take Talbott. You get Rosamund. We'll start with a little divide and conquer. I'll go first. You talk to Talbott. Then after I've congratulated Rosamund and talked to the Uptegroves a second I'll sashay over to Talbott. We'll be gone before Rosamund figures out who's where. After that you're on your own, bud. A mother's love can only go so far."

Miracle shivered, a thrill of tension at this wild, crazy talk. For a second he thought on the firm kiss Talbott had given his mother at the graduation picnic. Here she was warning *him* about Rosamund Uptegrove, and *she*, Martha Miracle, was married and a mother, *his* mother. Should he be an accomplice in this? Where was she heading, anyway?

Martha stepped from behind the tree. Miracle passed a hand over his hair and followed.

In the bare space before the trailer, Willie Uptegrove wrestled with the tripod of cascading roses. Big Rosie sat on a folding chair nearby. With a copy of the *Argus* she fanned

Bradford Uptegrove, whose head was tucked between his knees. No one else was in sight.

"Hoo boy," Big Rosie said, waving at Martha with the paper. "Is she hot to trot." She raised a paper cup.

"We came to offer congratulations," Martha said.

"Too late," Rosie said breezily. "She's off with Talbott Marquand. Now Miracle there, *he* might do us a favor, if he could get this lummox in his car and home." She poked her son. Bradford groaned.

"I'm not giving Bradford Uptegrove over to anybody," Willie said. "Especially no Catholics and no Miracles. They'd have him out on the road and pumped up with liquor in less time than it'll take him to sober up."

"Hear, hear," Bradford said. He did not raise his head.

They helped Bradford into the Uptegrove's Lincoln. Willie and Big Rosie climbed in. They drove away, bouncing across the ruts, roses trailing from the half-closed trunk. Miracle and Martha were left standing alone in the sawdust, Miracle in a dirty white T-shirt, Martha in her brilliant red dress, while the fair's last strings of bulbs bobbed and flickered overhead.

CHAPTER IV

Fool for Love

A WEEK LATER Martha was churning fresh-boiled tomatoes through a food mill when Grandma Miracle dumped the mail on the kitchen table. "Looks like a wedding invitation," Grandma said. "Now I wonder who's getting married this late in the summer? I ain't heard of no weddings except for that Skaggs girl, she's a shotgun, she ain't got the time to print up an invitation and she ain't got the money anyway." She held the cream-colored envelope to the window. She pulled a bobby pin from her bun and pried its tines apart with her teeth. She stuck it in the envelope and tugged at the flap.

"Grandma! That's my mail!" Martha snatched the letter from her mother-in-law's hands.

"Listen, honey, if I wanted to find out what was in that envelope I'd find it out. I'd just rather do the looking in front of your face instead of having to buy beer for the post office clerk or waste good whiskey on that worthless Ossetta. What

are you doing getting mail anyway? You're a married woman."

"There's no law saying married women can't get mail."

"I never got a piece of mail in my life that wasn't somebody
asking for something I couldn't afford to give. Open it." She
waved a gnarled hand. "Go on, I'm interested."

Martha peeled back the flap. "It's from Talbott Marquand,
Grandma. Would you like to read it?"

"You got no need to get so huffy." Grandma Miracle
grabbed the table edge and pulled herself to her feet. "You
read as long as you like. I don't need to know no more, and if
somebody don't get that juice in the jar it's going to get too
cold to seal."

It was an invitation, handwritten, for a drive. He needed
somebody to show him the territory, and everybody else had
turned him down.

Grandma Miracle filled a jar with juice and screwed on the
lid. "You'll say no," she said.

"No to what?"

"To whatever bullshit he's feeding you. I knew the second I
laid eyes on him at that picnic he was bound to go after
somebody. I just couldn't figure who it was. I figured Rosamund Uptegrove, but I guess Big Rosie's proved too much for
a Detroit Yankee to swallow. Can't say as I blame him there."
Grandma turned around, her chin tucked into the folds of her
neck. "I can see why it's you. He's a wife-breaker, that's his
kind, probably keeps count of the couples he's broke up. You
still got your looks and you got more fire than all them
Uptegroves piled in a pot."

"Grandma, I don't know what you're talking about. If he's
after me it's because he thinks there's money to be had somewhere. Though where he got that idea is beyond me." Martha

81

fixed her eyes on the pair of cardinals feeding in the sunflower stalks outside the window.

The old woman slouched on one hip, a steaming jar of juice clutched in a jar grip. Martha felt her gaze and she refused to meet it. Let her wonder, she thought, and high time. She stuffed tomatoes in the grinder and turned the handle as noisily as she could.

"I know my son's a pill," Grandma said, the moment Martha stopped churning. "He's a Miracle. I knew his father and his father's father and the father before that, a little, and every last one of 'em a trial and a cross to bear. At least you got that excuse—you never knew 'em, before Bernie. But they're your family, his family and your own, and you took 'em on of your own will. That might have been a mistake, I don't know. He's thirteen years older than you, I know that, and he's got the Miracle heart, you can tell it in his face. He'll be dead before you, long before you. Look at me. Why do you think it is that those Miracle men put our names on that mausoleum forty years before we're dead? They want to make sure we'll follow 'em to the grave, that's why. I still wonder if Bernie's father drowned in that river or if they scared his heart dead when they threw him in the trunk of that car. I guess it don't make no difference now, but you mark my word—your time'll come, soon enough, you'll be free as a jaybird with twice as much money. For now, you're a married woman. You might not like that—I don't know—I can't answer that for you. But you got married all the same, just like I done it and every woman that's got a heart does it. Now you got to make the best of it. That's what a woman's got to do, make the best of the mess this world's in. Because if she don't do it, I ask you who will. I got to ask that."

Martha turned around. Grandma Miracle gathered a wad of snuff into puckered lips and spat it into a pail of tomato skins and pulp. "I'll leave you to your juice," Grandma said. "You do it better than me anytime." She tilted her head to repin her bun. "You can count on me to keep my mouth shut. You do what you think best. You're a Pickett; you will anyway." She stumped from the kitchen, leaving Martha puzzling over the last boiling tomatoes of August, the cream-colored envelope tucked in her apron pocket.

* * *

Talbott picked her up the next Saturday, on a day when Bernie was gone to Louisville to meet with his distributors, and when Miracle was at the Inn. Really, she hadn't planned it that way. It just happened, in the way things do, she thought as she dressed, when they're meant to be.

She reminded herself that she was a married woman. She chose a dress, a white cotton pleated affair, old-fashioned for 1967, but cooler than pants and more respectable than shorts. In the bathroom mirror she adjusted her hat, a broad-brimmed straw hat with a wide scarlet sash, loaned for the summer by Rosie Uptegrove to protect Martha's fair complexion from freckling. It was an old-fashioned hat, it went well with the dress—too well, really, for a woman married twenty-three years. Twenty-three years! She considered. She repinned it, at an angle.

She watched the Mustang enter the drive, watched Talbott stop to wipe at a smear of dirt on the polished red paint. She wondered if he really was single, as Big Rosie assumed. She thought it unlikely. He seemed as solid as his waistline, dressed in clothes his wife bought to stay forever slightly out of style. Only his hat was unfaithful, a funny plaid hat with a feather tucked in its band. She could hear his wife's objections. He must have bought it on the sly.

She met him in the drive. The gravel burned through her

thin sandals and she found herself wanting to escape this
valley in a way she'd not allowed herself to admit in years.
She imagined them conspirators, hats tilted against prying
eyes. She closed her eyes and sank into the seat. Through her
pleated skirt the upholstery burned and stuck at once.

"Have you been to the mountains?"

She opened her eyes. "These *are* the mountains, in case
you hadn't noticed."

"No, I mean higher up. Eastern Kentucky. Past Lexington.
It'll be cooler there."

"That's a two-hour drive. I thought you wanted to look at
the country around here."

He shrugged. "You've got someplace else to be?" She said
nothing. "Escape to the mountains!" he cried. "East!" This,
she could see, was his notion of high adventure.

They shot through Lexington without stopping. In town
Talbott kept his eyes fixed on the road, as if worried that
someone might see him. They rode high over a viaduct, then
down, past shanties with tin roofs. On their stoops black
women rested spreading chins on thick hands, stirring the air
with funeral parlor fans and marking the progress of that fancy
car.

In a few minutes they left the city behind. Talbott pushed a
button. The car's top glided back. He drove carefully, so
carefully she felt he drove to avoid talking. She herself had
nothing to say and felt like saying nothing. She imagined the
mountains, where she would ride with cool air full in her face.

He wore no ring but he was married, she was as certain of
that as of her own husband. She thought on the source of her
certainty. It came, she decided, from *his* certainness, his
man's knowledge of that most perfect of excuses waiting in the
wings. She had that for an excuse, if it came to that; and as it
had to come, was coming, to that, she realized how ridiculous

84

she was. Her friends would worry, then talk, in their shrill, Southern voices, and they would be right to talk. She was old enough to know where this sort of thing led, and where it didn't, couldn't, lead. She pictured and heard her friends talking right now, as she headed to the ephemeral mountains.

She leaned forward to speak, to thank Talbott for the drive and to ask politely to turn back. She would say, the next day, that it was the heat, though she knew it was something more than that.

"Look," he said.

Ahead a bank of Queen Anne's lace bloomed with gold-finches. He slowed and honked. The flock scattered, fluttering black and yellow against the hot blue sky.

She turned the mirror to adjust her hat against the sun. She settled into her seat.

At a fork he turned left. The road narrowed. The shoulder gave way to a wall of vines sheared to the shape of the passing cars. Tentacles of sweet trumpet vine reached from the wall, slapping at the windshield. Each breath felt as if somewhere nearby a forest fire burned, robbing the air of oxygen and leaving only heat. She imagined the animals of the forest gathered by the roadside to savor the rush of a passing car.

Where the walls of vines broke the faces were all white now, thin and pale as winter moonlight. At road cuts the tangle of vines gave way to black gashes that crumbled coal onto the asphalt.

They crested a hill and dropped in looping curves to a river bottom. The road took a sharp turn and they entered a town.

The town was a mile long and a roofbeam wide. The houses backed up to a cliff and opened to the river and the single street, jammed with people. He pulled into a service station, a small whitewashed castle with crenelated turrets and a single pump. "Lost," he said. "Though we could turn around."

85

"It's fine," she said. "I don't have to be back 'til late."
She went inside, searching to escape the sun.

When she returned the car was gone. Standing in the sun
with the attendant and the clustered children and the barking
dogs, she felt exactly how alone she was. For twenty-odd
years she had dodged that knowledge. Now it fought its way to
the front of her heart. She thought back to the bitter June fight,
three months after Miracle's birth, when for no reason she
could put a pen to she knew that the heat of first love she'd felt
was no longer there and would never return, not with Bernie.
Since that night it had only been a matter of waiting.

Talbott pulled up then, profuse with apology. He had
moved the car to avoid blocking the pump, and had to drive to
the edge of town to find a space big enough to turn around in.
She took his arm for the walk to the car.

The town disappeared in a shimmer of heat before the first
bend, then the desolation began. Life vanished. Shovels had
turned the earth upside down, the black, coal-rich seams above
leaching color into the blue clay below. Mounds of earth
eroded into fabulous creatures threatened to swoop onto their
heads. With no forest for shade, the heat blasted from the coal-
blackened earth until she grew light-headed, separated from
her sweating body. She felt at peace, at home, for the first time
since she'd stepped from her cool kitchen; maybe for the first
time since she'd held Bernie's hand, a moment after they'd
married, and arched her eyebrows to his wink.

They left the mines as quickly as they had come upon them.
The road twisted upwards like a sidewinding snake, climbing
the spine of a ridge at an angle that pressed her back into her
seat and lifted her eyes to the sky. The pavement broke, then
ended at a sudden pothole. A swirl of gray dust rose behind
them.

They passed a shack, where skinny children with hair white

86

as sunlight rushed at the clearing edge pumping their fists. He honked. She like him for that.

The light slanted at their backs when they crested the ridge. Gravel gave way to ruts. He braked at a curve; they were swallowed by their own clouds of dust. She coughed and he stopped the car to wipe his eyes.

They might have been waiting since creation, the faces that lined that porch. They appeared through the settling dust, like spirits made visible by a thin coating of dirt. At the far end of the clearing a square frame church squatted before a single spreading oak. The road ended at a graveled turnabout.

Every living person was gathered on the single porch, which ran the length of the shacks. The men sat in clean overalls and white shirts, their hands planted on their knees. The women stood in faded print dresses, their children at their sides. They stood still and unblinking as for a photograph and in the still summer heat Martha caught the scent of Ivory soap. It was Saturday night.

He parked the car—it was as long as the shacks were wide. He stepped down. She did not want to get out but it was the end of the road; where were they going if not here? And to drive the length of the porch, under those eyes, to circle the turnabout without so much as an acknowledgement—that was as impossible as the thought of snow. She stepped from the car and shook the dust from her dress.

The men nodded, slightly. The locusts thrummed and a gust stirred in the trees but in her ears there was only the beating of her heart and the metallic tick of the cooling engine. Could these people talk? Could she talk herself? she wondered, in this silent place at the end of the world.

"Cafe's open," the man nearest them said.

There was a sign, she saw it now, weatherworn and pocked with birdshot. They moved toward it. There was no "no" in

87

that clearing. Time was the only excuse, and that was no excuse here.

Inside the dark pressed welcome as a damp cloth against her skin. A long bar ran down one side of the room, backed by a cracked mirror. To one side a rainbow of neon arched over the playing compartment of a jukebox. A dark square of floor framed a pale circle worn by dancers' feet. Martha sat away from the jukebox. Talbott crossed to the bar to order.

The men moved in from the porch. In the dark room they peered at her like raccoons from a knothole. The older men moved straight to the bar before turning to look at her, but the young men—the *young* men!—eyed her from the door, before turning their heads in a slow circle to check for her companion.

She had worn her hat inside to protect herself from curious stares. Now she pulled the pins that held it in place and set it on the table. The red sash drooped over her legs.

Talbott stood at the bar, his foot propped on its brass rail, his funny hat tilted at an angle that made the feather stand out. She was sorry that she so clearly belonged to him. Otherwise she might belong to these people. One of the pale young men might approach her, talking to her in a sharp twang whose words she would not need to understand, and out of place and time who knew what she might do? Could do? A high school memory returned: an evening waiting for a call that never came.

He brought her beer and a sandwich soaked in grease from its slab of ham. He excused himself to the men's room, apologizing for leaving her alone. She busied herself pouring her beer until he was off.

At the bar the cafe owner brought out dice. The younger men drifted to the bar and ordered beers. A ruddy boy with a washboard stomach and a painter's cap fed quarters to the jukebox, playing plaintive songs sung by women backed by slide guitars. He leaned his buttocks against the jukebox, his head bent and swaying in time with the music. Between songs he sipped his beer and smiled at her when she gave him the chance.

They all looked alike to her, these men, all glittering dark eyes and dull brown hair, in need of sunshine and a hot meal. All shared some angle of pale jaw or nose until she felt as if she were a stranger amid an immense extended family's reunion.

Only the ruddy-complexioned boy at the jukebox looked different. She pretended to adjust the hat's sash while looking over the brim. In the poor light she imagined his hair was blond, bleached pale by the sun.

A snappy tune came over the loudspeaker and she found herself tapping her foot. The ruddy boy looked at her and smiled. It was like marrying Bernie: she was out on the floor before she could say no.

She was not herself, she might say to the women in New Hope and Mount Hermon, though she felt more herself than she remembered ever feeling. It was the heat; it was the drive, so far from home; it was the blond lights in his hair.

He was a good dancer. They moved like a dream, she remembered fancy moves from a high school class, she used her feet and kept her eyes somewhere behind his back and shy of the men at the bar. For three minutes she belonged to him, showing off for eyes she hoped were looking.

Then it was over. He took her hand and she dropped his, she left him standing, she was alone at her table. She sat with her back to him and the bar, watching the curved arm in the jukebox travel under the rainbow, to the next selection.

The dice no longer rattled. The room sat quiet as a pasture before a July storm. The owner grumbled something under his breath. His neighbor laughed. Outside the cafe she heard the evening chatter of the birds and the shrill hum of the tree frogs. She leaned her head against the wall and closed her eyes. When Talbott moved from the shadows she rose and offered him her arm.

Outside the sun slanted through the trees. The women had moved with their children from the porch to the steps of the church, whose doors were open. They took her in with a single glance. She sat quickly, folding her hands in her lap. Circling the turnabout she felt in their brown eyes a mixture of envy and jealousy and fear that was as close to hatred as anyone could get in half an hour, closer than those first terrible days after her marriage to Bernie, when she was alone in New Hope and the life she'd left in Mount Hermon could have been a universe away. She wanted to leave the car, join the women on the steps and explain: the car; the heat; Talbott's wife; the dance, about which somehow she was certain they knew. Her head turned slightly, as if invisible threads connected her eyes to theirs. They looked at her, unsmiling.

The car passed the cafe. The ruddy boy stood on the steps. In this clear evening light his hair lay across his forehead, as flat and dull brown as a sparrow's back. In his hand, at his side, she saw her hat, the ribbon a red gash against his blue overalls. Talbott did not see him. She did not turn her head.

They regained the gravel, then the pavement. The sun slipped into a bank of clouds and the sky glowed like fire opal.

"You could have gotten us into a fight," Talbott said.

"I'm sorry."

"No, that's OK. I liked knowing I was with you. Every man in the place had his eyes on you and they all knew you were with me. I haven't felt like that in a long time. Maybe ever." He turned his head to look straight at her. "The bartender told me only fallen women came inside that place.

He actually used those words: 'fallen women.' " He rested his hand on her knee.

They inched down the ridge. At sharp curves he used both hands on the wheel, leaving a cool print of sweat on her knee. On straight stretches he replaced his hand.

They came to the mines. He slowed and turned down a gravel lane. Overhead the Milky Way arched like a sequined shawl against the velvet sky. He parked, tossing his hat in the rear seat. The ruined earth rose around them, barren and black; the air hung stale. They might have parked among the craters of the moon.

He moved to the back seat without speaking. She followed. On her knee his hand was moist and cool. She leaned her head back. Against the sky she framed like a moving picture the image of her dancing, a slow and elegant foxtrot to the twang of the slide guitar . . . she kept her eyes closed.

* * *

Back on the road, they drove in silence. They passed the crenelated gas station, empty and dark and still. No one walked the street; the crowd that day might have been ghosts. Where the road turned a caution light blinked, a yellow cat's eye against the black mass of the mountain.

The land flattened. Lights appeared through the trees, barnyard mercury lamps, surrounded by haloes of swarming moths.

He cleared his throat. "I have a wife."

She raised a finger. "The lightning bugs are beautiful tonight," she said.

Then the sky glowed, the fluorescent glow of Lexington, and they were back among the tin-roofed shanties, over the viaduct, into the city, the only car on the streets.

Back in New Hope, he stopped in the lane below the

Miracle drive. The house was dark. To the west the tanks and guns of Fort Knox lit the sky as brightly as sunset.

In the desperate grind of the katydids, in the touch of coolness under the warm air, she felt a hint of fall. She shivered. He laid a hand on her arm. "When can we get together again?"

In the dim light his blond hair seemed so ordinary and defenseless it pained her to look at him. He stirred a part of her that years before she had left behind for dead.

But then who was she? A stranger on the empty lane in front of her own house, a foolish woman with too much explaining to do.

She squeezed his hand. "I enjoyed the ride." She shut the car door carefully and entered her kitchen, alone.

CHAPTER V

In Between

SUMMER PASSED into fall. The hills flamed with scarlet sumac and gold hickory and an occasional bright red sugar maple. In the morning air the walls of the valley pressed in on Miracle as he went to work. He felt as if he were walking in an open bowl of flame. The mist from the river rose to blend with the smoke left from the Fort Knox firing practices, coloring the western sky gray. Miracle thought that hell must look something like New Hope: with the colors and the smoke and the rumble of the guns behind the hills.

Days were tense. Bernie never referred to the fair while making it perfectly clear that a son who sided with his mother in an argument violated the most basic principles of human decency and social order. On top of that Miracle had not seen or spoken to Rosamund since the night of the fair.

The fair ran in Miracle's mind long after the ferris wheel folded and the trees flamed red. Big events had happened, big in his life anyway. For a while Miracle waited for big changes to result.

But nothing changed, not for Miracle anyway. At lunch Talbott came to the Inn like always, to eat his pickled sausage and crackers and beer. Bradford Uptegrove talked about what a dog LaHoma Dean was and dated her every Friday night. Rosamund was nowhere to be seen, but on Saturday nights Talbott bought Wild Turkey and Asti Spumanti.

Only Martha had changed, and she made no attempt to conceal it. Miracle decided that either Bernie was blind or he was deliberately ignoring her. Working in the kitchen she sang little tunes, "Paper Moon" and "Tea for Two" and "Barbara Allen." She wore Sunday clothes around the house and put on lipstick in the mornings. Once Miracle found her staring into her bureau mirror, her head tilted to one side and resting in the cup of her hand.

Miracle mistrusted these changes. Something was afoot that he should be fearing and fighting . . . then Rosamund Uptegrove left for Nashville, and in the misery of the moment Miracle put thoughts of his mother from his mind.

Miracle and Rosamund hadn't been speaking, or at least Miracle hadn't been speaking to *her*. Rosamund seldom spoke first to anybody, and Miracle could not really say she wasn't speaking to him now. He expected somehow that she would say good-bye to him before she left. In one plan she came to the driveup window alone, apologizing for ignoring him and asking to meet at the mausoleum at midnight. In another plan she sent a note through Bradford, asking Miracle to meet below the bridge. She would reveal that she had been saving herself for Miracle. She might give herself to him then; at least she would plead with him to visit her in Nashville.

On the evening before Rosamund left for Nashville she drove up to the driveup window. Miracle was alone behind the

94

bar with no customers but for Estill Mallory and a farmer from the near side of Strang Knob, trying to make two beers last the night. Miracle's heart leaped when he saw her at the window. He leaned out over the little shelf that stuck outside the driveup window.

It was the last warm evening of the year. The air held fall and Rosamund was dressed for it, wearing a gold scarf wrapped gypsy-like around her black hair, and a cashmere sweater. She drove Talbott's Mustang, with the top down. She was alone.

"Hi, Miracle," she said. "Two fifths of Asti Spumanti."

He ducked inside. The shelf was empty of Asti Spumanti and he had to search the stockroom. He emerged with dust balls clinging to his clothes. She drummed her fingers on the window. "Add a fifth of Wild Turkey to that, please," she said. He got the bourbon.

"Twenty-four ninety-five," he said. She gave him a fifty. As he changed the bill he saw in the mirror a little trail of dirt stuck against his ear.

Faced with a topless Mustang his courage wilted. At the picnic he had been moved to ask Rosamund to meet him at the bridge, but then he had thought of them on even terms. Now she drove Talbott's car and was on her way to being a star in Nashville. He moved back to the window on reluctant feet. "When are you leaving for Nashville," he said.

"Tomorrow. I'm stocking up."

"They have liquor in Nashville."

"I know that. But I've developed a taste for this Italian stuff. Who knows where I can find it there. Besides, there I wouldn't be able to buy it from *you*." She took her change from his hand and she was gone.

* * *

95

More often than not, when Martha saw Talbott he was with someone else. She saw him on the Jackson Highway in front of Mallory's Merchandise, talking with Estill about his tool stock. Or she saw him at the construction site as she waited at the levee turnabout for a car from the south side of the river to clear the bridge. Sometimes she pretended a car was coming when there was none in sight so she could sit at the turnabout, watching Talbott from a distance. He was easy to pick out. His was the only blond head in the lot. When he wasn't bare-headed he was wearing the jaunty hat he'd worn when they drove to the mountains. She'd said she liked it, one morning when he wore it to her house. After that he wore it whenever he came to see her.

Sitting on the levee watching him was dangerous. With only a little craning of his neck Bernie could see the turnabout through the Inn windows. But every encounter she had with Talbott was dangerous, and she thrived on the danger. In chance meetings (not so chance, really, since they plotted where each would be and arranged their coincidences) she felt herself talking too loudly, gesturing too much and too widely. She would glance around the room, searching for his eyes, to find them already on her, his steady blue gaze meeting her own in a way that Bernie's had never done. With Bernie that gaze had been a puzzle, then a challenge. With Talbott it was the mutual exchange of desire, pure and simple.

Sitting at the turnabout, watching Talbott, Martha remembered those years with Bernie. Now they hardly seemed long at all. Instead they had passed faster than memory. One day Miracle was a baby, and she and Bernie were beginning to set into their hard and fast ways. The next she was throwing Miracle's graduation party on the banks of the Knobs Fork, and flirting, yes, flirting, with a married Yankee contractor. Did this happen because it had to happen, its time had come,

96

and anyone would do? Or because Talbott Marquand appeared, the right man at last, with his blond hair and Yankee ways? The question haunted her as she sat on the levee, waiting for an imaginary car to clear the bridge, watching Talbott climb in and out and among the muck and men and bulldozers.

It was risky, but it was better than waiting at home. There she never knew for certain when he would appear. He would promise to come in the morning, when Bernie and Miracle were off to work. Then there'd be a crisis at the site and she'd sit for an hour, two hours, drinking coffee until her nerves sang before she gave up on his coming. Or Bernie would return after the morning rush to work at home on his accounts. From the kitchen window Martha would see Talbott drive slowly up the Jackson Highway, pausing for a moment before her own drive; and, seeing Bernie's Rambler, speed on.

On mornings like that she snapped at Bernie and Miracle for no reason. Once when Bernie asked in his rough, joking way if she had ants in her pants, she ran from the house to the barren garden rather than let him see her cry. She stood in a drizzle, overlooking the river valley to the gray outline of Strang Knob, until she heard the Rambler start and drive away.

More than once she and Talbott and Bernie were together, just the three of them. One especially awful day Bernie returned to fetch a checkbook or a ledger or some trivial object he'd left behind, to find Talbott sitting at the kitchen table, calmly drinking the coffee Martha had thrust into his hands when she saw Bernie drive up. They'd acted as calm and unflustered as if nothing at all were amiss. Bernie had asked after the construction; Talbott replied that it was fine, that a man had to get away from time to time and he'd felt like taking a walk. Bernie had nodded, sympathized. Martha believed he suspected nothing, but he sat to coffee, twiddling his fingers, scratching at his ears, smoking.

Over Bernie's head Martha's gaze caught and lost Talbott's. She was afraid that if she met her lover's eyes too long that she would laugh, or break into tears, or that Bernie, even thick-skinned Bernie, would feel the longing passing from her to Talbott and back. She stared out the window, at the cardinals pecking at the sunflower heads she'd hung in the bare redbud branches.

When Bernie rose to go he offered Talbott a ride. Talbott accepted. Martha shook his hand (Yankee Talbott always shook the women's hands, even from that first day at Miracle's graduation picnic). She watched from the window, her hand tingling. They crossed the drive together, her lover and her husband. The cardinals, startled from their roost, fluttered to the top branches of the neighbor's hackberry, two gashes of fresh-drawn blood against the gray November sky. Watching the men go, Martha was overwhelmed by despair.

But there were other mornings, when Bernie left town for the day and Miracle was stuck at the Inn. Talbott would appear at the back door, having snuck from the rear of the pool hall along the L & N line to the river, and from there up through the fields. Then they would fall on each other, taking no time for explanations.

They went to Martha and Bernie's bedroom, where if Bernie returned they would hear his tires on the drive or his feet on the doorstep and have the chance of regaining enough clothes and respectability to avoid a confrontation. Opposite her bed there hung two wood mosaics, presents from Grandma Miracle at Martha and Bernie's wedding: the Sacred Heart of Jesus on the left, with rays of red cedar emanating from his dark walnut chest; and Mary Mother of Sorrows on the right, with seven swords of palest maple stuck in her rich cherry heart. Under their beatific gaze, Martha and Talbott made love.

It was only love, at first. After Bernie's hard, angular joints Talbott was thick and substantial. Martha's thumb and forefinger encircled Bernie's wrist with an inch to spare. With Talbott her whole hand rested like a child's in his own. Bernie's skin was scaly and red and raw, by blood inheritance and from years of work. Talbott was blond and fair and smooth as he could afford to be. Lying with him she took her greatest pleasure from looking at, and touching, as lightly as she could, his fair, thick body.

It was love; then she added hope. She felt sharp as swords the discoveries that were happening from within. She was forty-five years old, for more than twenty years she had lived with a man who begrudged her love and with whom she begrudged her body in return. With Talbott's every visit that part of her tucked at the back of her heart—the part that *felt*— emerged a little farther into the light.

She had hopes for this new, strange woman, emerging from an old and familiar self. At first she ignored her hopes. Then she fought them, or tried to forget them. It was useless. Wherever she'd been since she'd married, her heart was taking her in a new direction now, from which there was no return.

As surely as she came to hope, she saw Talbott come to fear. After sex their sweat cooled quickly in the chill November air. Then she saw the fear in his eyes. Without asking she knew why it was there.

They both felt the fear of being caught, of course. New Hope would have proof that Martha was the woman that for years they'd known her to be. Talbott stood to lose less, but his professional standing would be damaged among the Kentucky connections who arranged just the sort of country contracts that brought him to New Hope and gave him his excuse to flee Detroit.

But Talbott had a man's fears: He feared her love. He brought her roses once, roses in November! She threw her arms around him, overwhelming him with her surprise and joy. He left early that day, muttering excuses about mud in the equipment. She hid the flowers in the fruit cellar, where they wilted in the dark.

After that she was careful to restrain herself. She indulged in her hopes when she was alone, before her bureau mirror. They came as a flood, too large and too wide and too deep for Talbott to understand that only a portion of what he felt from her was love for *him*. Beyond that what she felt was love, pure and simple, for herself: for the chance to love, after all these years, and to be loved, in whatever way, in return.

* * *

On a cool bright November day, Big Rosie pulled in the Miracle drive. Watching the Uptegrove's long white Lincoln roll up, Martha suspected that Talbott might have other reasons for the fear lurking in his eyes.

She had been thinking what to fix for supper. With Rosie at the door Martha decided on vegetable soup, because she could start it quickly and keep her eyes from Rosie's. Martha retrieved a jar of tomato juice from the fruit cellar. When she returned Big Rosie was already standing in the kitchen.

"Whatever I'm interrupting it can wait," Rosie said.

"I'm just making supper," Martha said. "Have a seat."

Rosie had taken to wearing stretch pants, something she'd seen in Lexington at the university. When she walked the seams hitched up her broad hips. She shrugged them down now and sat with an impatient hiss at the Miracle's big round

100

table. "I'm not going to beat around the bush, Martha Pickett," she said.

"I've never known you to." Martha sliced across an onion, turned it ninety degrees, sliced again.

"I've heard rumors—too many and too much to call it rumors. Martha, you know perfectly well what I'm talking about."

"I'm afraid I don't." Heat the oil, stir in the onions, chop the garlic.

"Are you going to stand there and make me tell you, when half of Mount Hermon and all of New Hope has been talking of nothing else for the last two months?"

"I guess so." Rosie settled in her chair. Martha heard the soft squeak of polyester against wood. She chopped at the carrots.

"You're a disgrace. It's *worse* than marrying Bernie Miracle, at least that was legal even if it was Catholic. You're a married woman and more than forty years old, Martha Miracle, do I have to remind you of that?"

The hiss and pop of the vegetables in the hot oil filled the silence. Martha finished chopping the carrots, dumped them atop the onions. "Nobody knows that better than me," she said at last.

"Well, then, why don't you act like it."

Martha faced about then, crossing her arms and pushing back a thin strand of red hair with the tip of her knife. "Rosie, would you please tell me what you're talking about?"

Confronted with a bald request Rosie wilted. She slumped in her chair, picked at a piece of lint on her pants. "Why, I'm talking about your—behavior," she said.

"Meaning?"

Rosie sighed, took up her purse. From a gold case she

extracted a cigarette. From deep in her purse she pulled a silver flask. "You don't mind?" Martha retrieved a glass from the drainer, set it with ice and a soft drink on the table. Rosie poured a belt of vodka over the ice, ignoring the soft drink. "Martha Pickett," she began. "My oldest and dearest friend."

"*Could* you stop using my last name?"

"My oldest and dearest," Rosie repeated. "I don't mind telling you that I have hopes for Talbott Marquand—"

"So it's Talbott you're talking about."

"—and my Rosamund. It's seldom enough that a man with clean hands and a little money comes through this town, and a mother can't be blamed for thinking of her daughter's welfare. I'm sure you'd feel the same, if your Miracle was a girl."

"I doubt it."

"He's been dating Rosamund, Talbott has. He's had patience and he deserves to be rewarded."

"I thought Rosamund was in Nashville."

Rosie took a long gulp of vodka, closing her eyes while she swallowed. "That don't—doesn't matter. He can visit her there."

"I'm sure he has, Rosie, if that's a comfort."

"I hope he has," Rosie said. "It's a marriage made in heaven, Martha Pickett, it's what I've prayed for and hoped for all these years." She flicked her lighter with a thick, rose-tipped finger. When she took the cigarette from her lips a bright red ring encircled the butt.

Martha unscrewed the lid from the jar and dumped the tomato juice in the pot. If she kept her mind and her hands occupied she might survive this afternoon without doing something stupid. She heard the ice tinkle as Big Rosie sipped her drink. "He's a jewel of a man," Rosie said. "He's kind and thoughtful. He brought Rosamund roses once, for no purposes that I could imagine. Roses, at this time of year! Can you imagine?''

''I can imagine,'' Martha said dully.

''He's the only thing that can get my Rosamund out of this cowtown and onto someplace that's as big as she deserves.''

''She's in Nashville now. That's not big enough?''

''And he's the only thing that could get this Nashville manure out of her head. I won't stand by idle while you ruin him for her,'' Rosie said. Her voice dropped an octave, to the tone she used when she talked religion, or gossip. ''I've waited for years for this man to come along. I told Willie, when I heard that contract was to be let, I said, 'Willie, I don't want to see any old pot-bellied good ol' boy come down here.' It took some influence to get that contract awarded out of state, and to a Yankee on top of that. It took money, Martha Pickett, and while that may not mean much to you on this side of the river to me it means time and work and sweat.''

''Willie's sweat,'' Martha said. ''Although I bet Willie could go a week without changing his shirt, for the work he does.''

''Don't you sass me, Martha Pickett. I'm telling you this for your own good. You might have been married by a Catholic witch doctor but you were married, I heard you say it, 'til death do you part, I stood up with you, I still remember how you begged and pleaded with me to be your witness, when nobody else would do it, and I said no, no ma'am, you'll be sorry for this and you said you'd use Ossetta for a witness if it came to that. I told you you'd be sorry for this and you are, and I stand here ready to give you my shoulder to cry on and are you grateful. No, ma'am, butter wouldn't melt in your mouth. Well, that's OK, Martha Pickett, you be as stubborn and *Catholic*''—she relished the word like a curse—''as you want. But I'm not going to give up my daughter's husband, I

103

am *not*. When Ossetta told me you'd been seeing Talbott Marquand—"

"So Ossetta told you."

"She did, but it could have been practically anybody else in this town. I must say I wasn't surprised, considering."

"Considering what?"

Rosie sucked on her cigarette, twice. "Considering your blood, and the crowd you've married into."

"Then what about Michael Miracle."

"What about him."

"He's been dating Rosamund, or mooning over her, anyway. You know that, Rosie, as well as me or better."

"He's been *seeing* Rosamund. Or maybe I should say Rosamund has allowed herself to be seen. That's all that'll come of that, I guarantee."

This sounded too familiar to Martha; she'd heard it all before, in stereo, from her own mother and father, in those short weeks between meeting and marrying Bernie. But Miracle was her son, after all, and a far sight better man than Rosamund Uptegrove deserved. Judgement and manners told Martha to keep her mouth shut. She asked the question anyway. "What have you got against him, Rosie? What would be so terrible about Rosamund and Miracle seeing each other?"

Rosie dropped her cigarette into the melting ice of her drink. On its quick hiss she stood. "It's in the genes, Martha Pickett. *His* genes. All those Baptist genes and Catholic genes that hadn't been mixed up for four hundred years and that ought never, really now, *never* have been mixed up at all. And he's got 'em both, you can read it in his face; he's in between, not here or there, just in between. I don't want my daughter mixed up with a man that's in between. I want to set her up with a man that knows where he's been and where he's going and that

104

has the money and the gumption to get himself there. And your Miracle does not meet that description.''

''Is that all.''

''That's enough, let's just say that.''

''Well, it's not enough.'' Martha removed her apron, slowly and deliberately. ''He's married, Rosie.''

''Who's married.''

''Talbott Marquand. He has a wife. In Detroit, as far as I can tell.''

Rosie shrugged down her pants. ''That's a low trick, Martha Pickett, when I come over for your own good, with only your own good in mind, and you resort to telling me—*stuff*, just to get back at *me*, for doing *you* a favor.''

''Maybe that's it. Maybe I am getting back at you by doing you a favor. But you know me well enough to know that why ever it is I told you, I tell the truth.''

''I don't believe you.''

''Believe what you want. You will anyway.''

Rosie stood still for a moment, a white mountain of doubt. Then she bent to her purse and snapped it shut with a decisive click. ''He'll divorce,'' she said, with the force and certainty of the midnight coal freight.

Martha opened the door. ''Nothing you, nor Bernie, nor Talbott can say will be enough to change my mind, Rosie. I don't know who told you all you've heard and I don't know or care how much truth there is in it. I do know that I'm going places I ought to have gone a long time ago. If you take my advice, which you won't, you'd send Rosamund to Nashville and tell her to sing her guts out, if that's what it takes. I don't like your daughter, Rosie Uptegrove. She's a priss and a prig and she's dragging my son along with no more care for him than if he were—'' She searched for the comparison, but only

105

one came to mind. "—a Yankee that she thought might give her money and a good time."

"There's a lot to be said for money and a good time," Rosie said. "If you ask me you could have used a lot more of both in the last twenty years."

"So life with Willie has been constant joy and excitement. Please leave, Rosie. Take your gossip elsewhere. I'm sure you'll find plenty who'll kill to hear it."

Rosie left. Martha left the door ajar and opened the windows as well, to air out the smell of Rosie's cigarette. In the chill November air she sat at the big round table, her head in her hands, taking stock.

If Rosie knew, everyone knew, or would know. No one would know for certain, but they would believe the worst. She was ready for that. She'd known it all along.

Whether she was ready for her lover's unfaithfulness—that was a different matter. She could hardly call him faithless, he with a wife in Detroit. He'd even tried to tell her about it—a little late, maybe, but he'd tried, and with all the upbringing of a Southern woman she'd refused to listen. She'd been unfair to Rosie, telling her to believe what she wanted, when she herself, Martha Pickett of the truthful ways, was deceiving her husband and lying to herself about Talbott and Rosamund. And about Miracle, her own son, a single boy, beginning to be a man, with every right to fall in love with a single girl his own age, without worrying about whether his mother's lover was going to steal his girlfriend away. She'd lied to herself about all that, as surely and completely as Big Rosie pretended before her own husband that she'd never touched a drink in her life.

Behind her the soup hissed and bubbled. She lowered the flame, then threw the cabinets open and banged down mixing bowls for cornbread. In that loud, angry moment she decided what to do: nothing.

She never told Talbott of Rosie's visit. The question of his marriage did not trouble her—they were both married. As for his visits to Rosamund—they were Talbott's affair. For herself, she knew this affair could go nowhere, at the same time that she knew she did not want it to end, not now, when she was awakening to something much larger than her love for Talbott. To leave him now would be to return to the inert stuff she'd been for more than twenty years. If she lied in not telling Talbott of Big Rosie's visit, these were lies of omission, not commission. She told no lies. She simply hugged the truth to her heart.

CHAPTER VI

Smoke and Mirrors

THE WEATHER TURNED. The river bottoms froze and thawed. On a cold day you could walk the river bank on a crust of frost; then the sun would emerge from behind the gray sheet of the sky and you'd be standing in muck to your knees.

Talbott came less and less often to New Hope because, Martha hoped, construction on the bridge had slowed. If she stopped to think on that, and on Rosie's visit, she knew there were more substantial reasons for his absence, but with Christmas approaching it was easy to stay busy. Martha made sure to stay very busy, too busy to think on the whys and wherefores of Talbott's absences.

On Christmas Eve Miracle and Bernie worked the Inn together. From Bradford, Miracle had heard that Rosamund was back in town, but only for the holiday. She had a demo tape arranged with a friend in Nashville, who could only get a studio the day after Christmas. Rosamund would leave Mount Hermon on Christmas night.

Miracle was miserable. Partly he was miserable because Rosamund had not called, partly he was miserable because after three months of being gone she could still make him miserable. He thought to call her, but shied away. Instead he sent letters, which went unanswered. If there were justice in the world, Miracle thought, surely he would have recovered from these fits by now. Yet on his trips to the north pilings (infrequent, now that it was winter) Rosamund haunted his memory with the persistence of the tank gunners firing on the artillery ranges behind Strang Knob.

On Christmas Eve the Inn was like times before Vietnam. No draftees stood at the bar; they'd been sent home for the holidays. Only the wind shook the windows in their frames. The war games behind Strang Knob were canceled for the night. The men at the bar argued about the war but they might as well have argued the price of tobacco. They argued the summer's race riots in Los Angeles and Detroit and Louisville, but on a cold Christmas Eve those events were as far away as Vietnam. They just made for good talk. Nobody really disagreed about anything, except religion. Regarding any other subject the assumption prevailed that south of the Ohio all white men (and black men of any count) agreed.

Miracle set himself up with a good supply of bar towels. Early on he learned that bartenders polish bars not from compulsive cleanliness but from a finely-honed instinct for self-preservation. Without a bar to polish, bartenders would soon be driven crazy by the sort of people who hang around bars.

Miracle was polishing the golden oak top of the colored bar when the driveup window buzzed. He crossed to it and flipped up the plastic square. He stuck his head into the foggy breath of a December night. It was Rosamund.

She seized his hand. "I've got to talk to you, Miracle," she said. "About Talbott. And—" she paused "—forever."

109

"OK," Miracle said. "Shoot."

"Not *here*!"

"You got a better idea? Your apartment in Nashville, maybe?"

"Come on, Miracle, I'm sorry if I haven't gotten in touch but there wasn't anything I could do. I've just been running around like a chicken with its head chopped off. Not a second free since I got down there."

"You could have stopped dating Talbott Marquand. That would have given you more free time." A second car pulled up behind Rosamund.

"Please," Rosamund said. "It's important, Miracle."

The driver behind Rosamund tapped his horn. "You're blocking the window," Miracle said. "Do you want something?"

"A bottle of Asti Spumanti."

"And a fifth of Wild Turkey."

"Miracle, stop it!" She shook his hand free. "Get me my wine."

He bagged her a bottle and stuck it through the window without leaning out. She leaned up to his hand. "I'll be back here when you close to pick you up," she said. "If you're not here, well, I'll know you don't love me any more." She cranked up her window and spun off into the Christmas Eve night.

Love? Rosamund Uptegrove mentioning love? Miracle was so taken aback that the next customer had to repeat his order, and still Miracle got it wrong.

By the time Miracle took up his cloth, his Uncle Leo had joined the other men. They formed a circle at one end of the bar, arguing in the way Miracle knew so well. Each man threw his opinion down with the force and certainty of God deliver-

110

ing the commandments. He assigned everybody else opinions counter to his own, then argued with himself for as long as they would listen. Pretty soon everybody would be hot under the collar, with a few choice names flying and a little elbow jostling for show. Listen long enough and they'd work their way back to where they started—everybody in agreement. They'd throw their arms around each other, buy a last round of beer, and stagger into the night. It was the Southern way to argue.

Things had reached their peak—with everybody glaring at each other and Leo starting in on the communists and civil rights—when Miracle saw Bradford stumbling through the crowd. He reached across the bar and seized Miracle's hand. "I'm in trouble, Miracle."

"So what else is new." Bradford's eyes were glazed over, his pupils hardly bigger than pinheads. He weaved in time with his words. Miracle sniffed. There was not a drop of liquor on his breath.

"It's LaHoma Dean," Bradford said. "We had a date. Christmas date. She says. She wants. She's got to get married, that's all she'll consider."

"So? You been talking about breaking up for six months," Miracle said. "Now's your chance. You've already told her how you feel about that."

"I got to go, Miracle. Get out. I'd go to California if I had the money. You can get me the money, hnnh? You must have lots of money around here. I bet you go through a thousand dollars on a night like this. Bernie'd never miss a couple hundred. Hnnh?"

"How can you not have the money? You've been working since July."

Bradford shrugged. "It just goes, Miracle. One thing and

another. A little tail, a little crystal. I've paid more money to Fort Knox GI's than Uncle Sam has. And now LaHoma Dean. She says she's *got* to get married. *Got* to.''

Understanding struck. Miracle shook his head. "You mean—''

Bradford slapped his hand over Miracle's mouth. "Not here, Miracle. Not *now*. Somebody'll hear. If her folks find out—if my folks find out—it'll be shotgun or run for me.'' Bradford laid his head on the bar. "I'll go to Nashville. I'll live with Sister, sweet, darling Sister. My sister the star. How'd you like to have a sister who's a star. Oh, God, Miracle, how in the hell am I going to get out of this one?''

Miracle looked around. Bernie was out of sight. Miracle pushed Bradford's head up. "The first thing you got to do is straighten up. I don't know what you're high on but you can't get high on it here. Bernie'll have you out on your ass in the time it takes you to figure out where you're going.''

Bradford jerked upright. "Let him try.'' He slammed the bar with his fist. Heads turned, all except Leo's, too deep in his argument to notice. "Any man who can't keep his own wife tied down ain't likely to be throwing *me* around.''

Miracle could count on one hand the fights he'd been in. He could count on his fist the fights he'd started. But it was Christmas Eve, and Rosamund was in town, and here came Bradford, drugged up and putting into words what Miracle had heard whispered, just loud enough for him to hear. He'd not believed it. He wouldn't believe it now. Quicker than thought, Miracle slammed his fist against the sharp edge of Bradford Uptegrove's teeth.

In the South, in the Inn, fighting was as contagious as summer flu. For a long calm moment Miracle stared at his Uncle Leo's face without really understanding how it got there, lying flat on the bar with one eye swelling shut and the

112

other roving the ceiling. In the second Bradford Uptegrove took to regain his balance, Miracle realized there were two fights going and that someone had laid Leo across the bar.

Miracle and Bernie collided at the flap that separated the white and colored bars. Bernie swept Miracle back with a wave of his arm, pushing him against the rack of bottles. Miracle was up and through the flap before it fell shut.

They were too late. Leo was on his attacker and already somebody was on top of Leo. Bernie waded into the bodies, to be caught by a fist—maybe even Leo's fist—and knocked against the bar. Bradford came weaving after Miracle, his lip dribbling a red trickle of blood. Bradford threw a fist. Miracle dodged. Bradford stumbled against the ornate oak pilasters of the colored bar.

The crowd thinned to the fighters, mostly Catholics. The Baptists hanging in the corners fled. Through moving bodies and flying fists Miracle saw Bernie, struggling to his feet. Bernie was angry and afraid at once, his square jaw slack and his eyes glancing about and his hands clutching and unclutching at his sides. From the direction of his father's glances Miracle knew Bernie was afraid not for himself but for the Inn, the building that was more Miracle than any single Miracle, the place that was his father and his grandfather and his great-grandfather in wood and copper and glass. Miracle leapt into the pile of bodies.

He didn't last long. He never saw who hit him. Later Miracle swore it was Bradford Uptegrove. At that moment Miracle knew only that the blow was from behind, and that it was something hard and heavy and solid. He pitched forward, his hands flailing and his vision blurred, his eyes losing focus slowly, like a binocular lens turned too far. He heard a loud crash, then a sound like the rush of the river past the bridge pilings in a March flood. The rush turned to a roar. Miracle

113

passed out, his head neatly framed against the hills and the rising (or setting) sun carved into the pale oak of the colored bar.

*   *   *

In Jessup County the Miracle Inn is the civilized bar, the bar where the money goes, when there is any, the bar that the other bar owners come to when they have somebody to impress. Over the years Bernie had made it clear that he did not allow personal differences to be settled on the premises. People who chose to fight were writing their own tickets out, and Bernie had a long memory.

To give Miracle his due, Bradford Uptegrove did in fact swing the beer mug that struck Miracle from behind. The crash that Miracle heard as he fell was the mug, torn from Bradford's hands by Leo and tossed at his attacker. But Leo had no time to compensate for his swollen eye. The mug floated past Bradford into the beveled mirror behind the white bar, that had mirrored soldiers at their Union and Confederate reunions and soldiers from the Spanish American and World Wars and Korea, that had seen Prohibition come and go and liquor legal and illegal enter the door, that had begun to see soldiers off to Vietnam, that mirror that had reflected Martha Pickett and her son and Talbott on the long night of the Jessup County fair— that beveled mirror shattered into ten thousand slivers of light, as if for a century it had waited patiently for a one-eyed cyclops to toss his mug.

The fight stopped, as quickly as it had started. Maybe it was fear of Bernie. Maybe it was the first bell at Assumption Church, sounding the call to midnight Mass. Most likely it was the realization, even through the pounding of arteries bursting with adrenalin and alcohol, that any man who fought on a floor covered with broken glass was likely to get his ass cut.

114

Men who a few minutes earlier had been pounding each other's heads, helped one another straighten ties and brush off dirt. More than one man turned to the mirror to straighten his clothes, only to find the mirror gone and in its place a starburst of a black hole.

Those who hadn't families to drive to Mass swept up glass and set up the chairs that had been overturned. One by one they left, muttering apologies and excuses to Bernie. In the confusion Leo disappeared.

Bernie propped his son on a chair. He ran his hand over Miracle's head, knocking shards of glass to the floor. He found no cuts but felt a goose egg rising from the nape of his son's neck. With a woman's tenderness he wiped clean his son's face. He wrapped the towel around some ice and draped it over Miracle's head.

Miracle opened his eyes. He saw Bernie, his anxious face peering into Miracle's own, from closer than Bernie had been since before Miracle had a memory to remember. Miracle struggled to sit upright. He felt his swollen head. His eyes swam.

"How are you feeling," Bernie said.

"Like I stepped in front of the L & N coal run."

"Good. I don't know if it's happened to you before, but if you're going to stay in this business it's got to happen to you sometime, you can't learn any other way." Bernie unfolded himself upward. "*If* you're going to stay in this business. I wish it hadn't happened here. I don't know why you can't learn your lessons in some two-bit bar joint instead of here, where you think you'd have some respect for the family."

Bernie picked at his sleeves as he spoke, staring not at his son but at the mirror shards littering the floor and picking, picking. "You don't understand what you have here. This place will be here after I'm gone and after you're gone. People might not remember you but they'll remember the Miracle name and they'll go to the Miracle Inn and have a drink on us whether they know it or not. They'll meet people and they'll have a few beers and maybe they'll get to where they don't feel so bad about themselves and the world. Someday maybe you'll understand how much that means."

He stood for a while in silence. Miracle waited for more. Bernie had heard, could not help but have heard, what Bradford had said about Martha and Talbott. He must know why Miracle had thrown the first fist, what had started that fight. Bernie must know something about Martha and Talbott, and knowing, surely he would say something.

Bernie said nothing. He laid the keys on the pool table. "Lock up," he said. "I'm meeting your mother at Assumption Church. If I'm not there God knows what she'll get into. If you're feeling good enough to talk back, you're well enough to lock up." Bernie left.

Miracle cursed himself. He might have said something to bridge the gap between himself and Bernie. He had the chance, back there on the chair, with Bernie looking at him as if he were a child again and had fallen and skinned his shin. Following Miracle's regrets came his pride, as fast and strong as the Knobs Fork after a July cloudburst, and his stubbornness. *He* had no call to say anything. *He* had never asked to run the Inn.

It was the pride and stubbornness of the Miracle blood, the blood that made them father and son and that kept them apart.

Miracle pondered this as he moved about the bar, turning off lights, counting the change and bills in the register. He moved slower than usual. It was past midnight by the time he banked the ashes in the stove and tapped the damper shut. He straightened himself slow as an old man—he still had the dripping towel around his neck. Behind him the door opened.

Miracle turned, already clearing his throat to ask the latecomer to leave.

Rosamund Uptegrove stood in the doorway, wearing the same blue chiffon and sequined dress that only last August had swept Miracle's breath away.

His breath was swept away now, and his heart, and his blood. He stood unmoving, unable to move, until Rosamund crossed the room and wrapped him in her arms.

She pulled him from his stool and thrust his head under the faucet behind the bar. Miracle found himself blessing the beer mug that had raised the lump on his skull and that had brought Rosamund to his side with cries of mercy. Florence Nightingale in blue sequins, gently toweling his red hair, Rosamund Uptegrove loved him more than ever. She loved him because she had saved his life.

She told her story as she patted his hair dry. She was angry with Talbott. From rumors and Big Rosie's hints she'd surmised his affair with Martha.

"Not that there was much guessing," Rosamund said. "Mamma doesn't leave much to the imagination."

Miracle picked at his sleeves, rolled them down, buttoned and unbuttoned his collar. "What business is it of hers anyway," he said finally. "I don't believe it. I don't believe a word of it."

"Well, it's true," Rosamund said.

"It is *not* true."

"Miracle, I *know*. I asked him. And at least he didn't try to lie his way out of it, I'll give him that much."

"So why are you still seeing him!" Miracle cried. He jerked his head up. His temples throbbed, his vision swam. He lowered his head.

"I'm *not* seeing him, dear," Rosamund said with cool logic. "I'm seeing *you*."

117

"You'll see him again."

"I might. I don't see how that's a concern of yours."

She was an Uptegrove, no doubt about it. Only Big Rosie's daughter could be quite so cool about matters that set Miracle's own Pickett heart on fire. Faced with her unflappable certainty, Miracle made his decision: he would play her way. He reached behind his head, grabbed her hand, and tugged her in front of him. "To hell with all of them anyway," he said, and pulled her into his lap.

Through long kisses his mind wandered. He suspected that Rosamund's attention had its source in some desire to spite his mother by seducing her son. Well, two could play that game. With the same spirit that led his mother to forge ahead with a doomed affair with a married man, Miracle quelled inner wisdom in favor of love and desire and a small measure of his own revenge: on Talbott, on his mother, on Bradford Uptegrove, for being so free and easy with his beer mug.

He forced his mind back to the present. He wrapped his arm around Rosamund's shoulder, shifting his hand so that it was in her long, dark hair.

"Not *here*," she hissed, but she stayed inside the curve of his arm.

"Don't move, not a finger," Miracle said. He rose and circled the room, pulling the shade at each window and turning out the lights. He stopped at the jukebox, dropped in a quarter, and punched up three Patsy Cline tunes.

He stood next to Rosamund. She leaned into him, her hair like spun coal bunched against his chest. She pressed the length of her body against him, half lifting him onto the pool table. She hefted herself onto his lap and undid the bottom buttons of his shirt while he fumbled among her sequins for her zipper. Before the heat of her purpose and passion his Catholic guilt wilted like plucked chicory in a July sun. On the

118

soft green baize of the north-slanting pool table, for the first time in his life, Miracle lost himself to lust and love.

Or tried to lose himself. According to what he'd heard, this was supposed to come naturally, without thinking. Miracle found himself thinking double-time, working harder than on any Saturday night at the Inn. In the midst of romance, in the middle of the longest kisses he'd ever known, his mind was drifting, no matter how he fought against it: off to his mother, to Talbott Marquand. Where was Talbott now? Up in Detroit, no doubt dividing his time between a third and fourth woman.

And here was Miracle, in his first try at honest-to-God, all-the-way sex. He knew what it was supposed to be like. He'd read books and magazines. They all agreed that the first time was the best time. Miracle found himself thinking that if this time was the best, he had a sorry sex life ahead. His pecker stayed limp, a flaccid jello wiener under Rosamund's hand. How could this happen, after so many nights of hoping and praying for just what had come to pass? Sex on the pool table at the Miracle Inn! Nobody would believe it. *He* couldn't believe it. Miracle put all his brain below his belt. Nothing happened.

In the middle of a tepid kiss Rosamund broke away. "Earth to Miracle," she said. "Come in please. What's wrong with you?"

"My head hurts too much," he said lamely. "We should make a date. Tomorrow night. I'll be better tomorrow night."

"I'll be in Nashville tomorrow night. Thank God." She slid from the pool table. "I'm not about to get Big Rosie on my tail for sitting and smooching in the Miracle Inn." Miracle looked crestfallen. Rosamund relented, laying her arms across his shoulders. "Cheer up, Miracle. I'll write, I promise, and tell you all about it. And you can come on down, sometime. You promised, remember? At the fair." She played with the hair at the nape of his neck, running her fingers across the lump, still rising. Miracle grimaced. She laughed and pecked his cheek. "That's what you get for fighting over women," she said. "See you down south."

She was gone before he could stand, out the door in a great clashing of chiffon. In Willie Uptegrove's Lincoln she spun from the lot, throwing gravel against the Inn windows, leaving Miracle standing alone on the splintered planks of the Miracle Inn, hugging his bony elbows to his chest and considering the jagged fragments of his reflection in the shattered mirror.

* * *

Standing in the Assumption Church vestibule Martha bent to the clear pane in the stained glass doors, to watch the priest lead his procession of servers to midnight Mass. They walked with the grace of penguins on land, the tallest and oldest boys who brought up the rear pushing and shoving as they marched up the aisle. She'd seen her first Mass from this same pane. The priest was older and fatter now, his prayers were in English, but the congregation still mumbled and the vestibule smelled as faintly and thoroughly of incense as ever.

Bernie laid his hand on her shoulder, so quietly and suddenly she jumped. When she looked at him she fell against the swinging door, so hard that faces in the rear pew turned.

Bernie had managed to tie his tie in the car mirror but patches of dirt spotted his coat and the red rose Martha pinned on him each Christmas Eve was squashed flat against his lapel. Under one eye his cheek swelled pink and green and the effect on Bernie's pale and bony face was close to leprosy.

Behind the bruises Martha saw the look of knowledge in his eyes. She could not know who told him or how, though she connected his look instantly and unmistakably with the bruise under his eye and the smudges on his coat. "Where's Mira-

120

cle?'' she asked, the easiest and least dangerous question she knew.

Bernie took her arm. "He is not in the grave or in jail or chasing after whoever it is he's fixed himself on climbing into bed with. He is at the Inn, where he ought to be on Christmas Eve, closing up the bar like I did when I was his age and where God willing his son will be on Christmas Eve when he is my age. Now sit down and we will pray for the family like the good Catholics we ought to be even if we ain't. God knows we need it.'' He guided her into the church, his grasp on her arm as weak as a child's, his step as tired and shuffling as the oldest man's.

CHAPTER VII

Promises, Promises

MIRACLE KNEW something was up when on Christmas Day Bernie asked him to chop wood. Hard work on Christmas Day had to be a mortal sin, and Bernie could be relied upon to know all the sins in all their degrees. Besides, Bernie never *asked* anybody to do anything. Either you did it or Bernie did it himself, conveying without words the fact that he was doing your job and doing a better job of it to boot. When Bernie made his request of Miracle, he'd made it politely, in language more likely to come from Martha than from anybody on the Miracle side of the family.

Miracle's breath came in clouds and under his coat his sweat sat in cold puddles. He had barely warmed up when Bernie came from the house to stand in range of Miracle's ax. Miracle held off chopping.

"I want you to promise," Bernie said.

Miracle leaned on the ax handle. The day was cold and

gray, colder than Christmas in the Knobs ought to be. The smoke from Bernie's cigarette rose straight up, without so much as a coil, until it passed Bernie's gray-flecked hair.

"Promise what," Miracle said.

"Promise me what I want." From his coat pocket Bernie pulled the silver flask, engraved with the initials of his grandfather, the man who built the Miracle Inn, and set his mausoleum on the biggest knoll in the Catholic cemetery. "Have a drink," Bernie said. Miracle drank, and handed the flask back to Bernie. "Keep it," Bernie said with a wave of his hand. "I got it from my father when I was your age. It was the only thing he ever gave me before he died. 'This goes to the Miracle that runs the Inn,' he said. It was the last thing he gave me, too, except for the Miracle Inn."

"Give it to me when you're ready to die, then," Miracle said.

"If you waited for that you'd never set hands on it. Leo would have it from my pocket before my butt was cold. Don't give me any shit. Take it. It's yours." Miracle stuck the flask in his hip pocket. Bernie stuffed his hands deeper in his pockets and stared at Miracle with a brown intensity. Miracle leaned his ax against the log he'd set upright and turned to look west to Strang Knob. "You promise?" Bernie asked of his son's back.

"I can't promise if I don't know what you want."

"You know what I want. I want to know that my son will follow me like I followed my father. I want to know that the Miracle Inn will stay in the family, instead of getting sold off to some no-count Yankee who wants to put in a Dairy Queen and a car wash. I heard talk already. Leo thinks Talbott Marquand's got the best ideas for running the place. If I turned it over to Leo, he'd have the place wrecked for the dime it cost him to call the wrecker. He won't say that now, but I know. I know by the look in his eye, I knew it the day they opened my father's will and they read where the Inn was to be all mine, only mine. My father did a lot of stupid things in his time and he paid for them I guess, but he knew what he was doing when he gave that Inn to me. And I know what I'm doing now."

Miracle did not turn around, even when he heard Bernie grind his cigarette beneath his heel. Bernie cleared his throat and spat. "So you won't promise."

"I can't promise to do something I'm not even half sure what is. I'll run the Inn when you need me. Next year—hell, I might be in college next year. I might get drafted. I might be in *Vietnam*, next year." I might be in Nashville, with Rosamund Uptegrove, he added to himself.

"Not if you're running the Inn. The Army won't draft a mother's sole support."

"I'm not my mother's sole support. You're my mother's sole support." Miracle picked up the ax. With a clean blow he split the log before him. "I hear they're talking snow. If I don't get this wood put up now we're not likely to get it up 'til we need it."

"You," Bernie said. At that voice Miracle stopped. He looked at his father in the gray failing December light. Bernie's face was bright red. On his nose the tiniest veins stood out.

"You, do what you think best," Bernie said. "You will anyway. That's what makes you a Pickett. I guess." He turned. "I got to go inside. I'm not up to stacking wood, not now." He shuffled to the house, picking his sleeves as he went.

Miracle chopped, hard, sure strokes, until he heard the thunk of the storm door closing. Then he buried his ax in a stump and sat, crossing his arms and keeping his back to the

124

Miracle house. Was it so much on Christmas Day, to promise a father what he wanted? For a week, or a month, or a year, Miracle could have made Bernie happy, and Bernie, a Catholic and a Southerner, was not a happy man by nature. It was little enough for a son to make a promise that a year later, with any good excuse, he could break. Lots of things changed in a year, even, just possibly, Bernie.

Miracle shook his head and stood. He pulled the flask from his pocket and lifted it to the gray sky. "To the family," he said, and drank.

* * *

Martha was never so aware of herself as an interloper to the Miracle family as when she bent to the stove. Whatever measure of acceptance she'd gained in twenty years she could lose in a moment, by putting bacon in the fried apples or leaving marshmallows off her candied yams. The feast would be set out on the table, the endless family lined up to feed. One by one they would pass her dish by. A sister-in-law might exclaim, "Well, I never. Hard-boiled eggs in the tuna salad! Martha Pickett, you always got a new idea," meaning, "Twenty years and she still lays a Baptist tuna salad!" Loyal Dolores would take a tablespoonful. At meal's end the table would be ravaged, littered with corpses of empty dishes. Only Martha's contribution would sit pristine, untouched except for her own helping and Dolores's daring tablespoon.

Talbott was gone, home to Detroit for Christmas. When he'd told her he was leaving, she'd thought of it as time to make a break. He would go away; out of sight, out of mind. She would compose herself and a speech for his return, when she would announce that it was over between them.

Then he left, and she found herself counting the days until

he returned; looking with longing at the telephone, knowing that she could find his number, she could call, if she wanted to be so brazen. Desire raged against good sense.

She had been in this place before, when Bernie Miracle asked her to cross the river. How often and how hard did a body have to endure lessons before it finally took them to heart?

When Bernie entered the kitchen, she was mixing up cara-mel icing for the jam cake she was to take to the Miracle family dinner. He stood under the bright kitchen light, passing nervous hands across his hair, cut like the stubble of winter straw. Martha noticed how gray his hair was, how much grayer it had turned in the last several months, or was that her imagination? She had been so swept up in Talbott, in the changes in her own life, that she'd hardly looked at Bernie in a longer time than she could remember.

He was smoking more and drinking more coffee, she knew that because she emptied the ashtrays and bought the Maxwell House. His cheeks were flushed, they'd always been that way, but now the blush stood out in two bright red roses against his skin. Above these the bruise from the Christmas Eve fight swelled blue and yellow.

But the icing was on the flame, and the memory of too many grainy icings served to too many Miracle women weighed on her hands, and though she could not remember the last time Bernie had approached her alone to talk she kept her mind and her eye on the bubbling pot.

"I want you to promise," Bernie said.

"Promise what?"

"That you'll be buried next to me. In the Miracle family plot."

With great deliberateness Martha dripped icing from her spoon into a bowl of water. She fingered the glob of sugar and

126

butter: too soft. She did not turn to Bernie until the icing was back over the flame. Then she spoke with no more heat than if she were bidding clubs in the Tuesday night bridge circle. "Bernie, I don't give a damn where I'm buried. You got my name on that gravestone, you put me there. That's as good a place as any, and with a view. Though given my druthers, I'd as soon be in the garden out back, if I had an opinion on the subject which I don't. Now let me finish my icing in peace. Please."

Bernie remained unmoved. "That's not the same as a promise, saying you don't care. I know you don't care. I care."

"Then do what you want."

"I won't be here to do what I want. You got to promise to do what I want."

"Bernie Miracle, I don't *got* to do what anybody wants. I do things because I want to do them, or because I think they're the right thing to do even if I don't want to do them."

"Which one's the reason why you stayed with me for twenty-three years, then."

In little plops and hisses the icing bubbled. Outside Miracle's ax fell on seasoned oak in a steady thunk.

Martha turned to face her husband. "I try to live an honest life, Bernie Miracle. If I have learned one thing it's that it's not easy to be a good woman or a good man in this world. You can stick your head in the sand or you can lift it out, but you can bet if you lift it out you're going to get things thrown at it. I could have stayed in Mount Hermon, you know that. I could have married a good Baptist boy and by now he'd have built me a nice split-level ranch house with an all-electric kitchen and a dishwasher. You could have married a good Catholic girl who'd have given you bean soup every Friday and all the children you wanted and then some. I married across the river, and I married into the Church, and I did both because I thought

127

they were the right thing to do. I have always thought that you did the same thing for the same reasons.

"You didn't know what you were getting into then, neither of us did, but we've figured it out, some, anyway, since. And you ought to know you can't ask me that kind of promise. Maybe once, twenty years ago. Not now. I've learned a little about myself, Bernie. I can't give you that promise any more than I could have married that nice Baptist boy with the split-level and the dishwasher. If I promised you I would be lying, I know that and you do too. Most of the time I can't figure out what's right or what's wrong. I'd be a fool to do the wrong thing when finally a time comes when I know what's right. So I won't promise, because I can't promise."

"A good wife would promise."

"Bernie, I *can't* promise, can't you see that?"

Bernie's hand passed over his hair, fingered his earlobe, touched the swollen place below his eye and rested there, kneading it lightly as if caressing the pain. "I wonder how much you love me," he said reflectively. "I wondered it then. I wonder it now. I guess I always will." He left the kitchen as quietly as he had entered.

If in twenty years he'd used the word "love," she couldn't remember it. Now when forced to say it, he asked for it in tablespoons or ounces or cups, measured out as surely as butter and brown sugar.

It's not *fair*, she wanted to cry. She stood pointing her wooden spoon like a weapon at the place where Bernie had been, until stirred back to life by the smell of her icing, ruining over the flame.

* * *

The rights and wrongs of it all stayed floating in the air, but about the facts of his situation Bernie won out. The next day, as he and Leo stacked cases of pink champagne at the Miracle Inn, Bernie dropped a case and sat on it, gray and glassy and clutching his side. His heart stuttered once, then twice again, quick as boxer's punches, while Leo shoveled his brother's limp body into the cab of his pickup and careened across the river to Mount Hermon Baptist Hospital.

Leo might as well have taken his time. Long before he pulled into the emergency dock, Bernie's heart had stopped, as still and dead as the river bottoms on a clear cold winter night.

CHAPTER VIII

Free at Last . . .

SHE HAD WANTED to be free; now she was free.

Across four days Martha sat with the casket from nine a.m., when the funeral home opened, until the last visitor had left and there was only Grandma Miracle and herself and her son. She would like to have believed that she stayed from love, but her conscience allowed no part of that. She stayed from guilt, and anger, and fear of feelings that she kept at bay by immersing herself in the Catholic way of dying.

Bernie died on Thursday; Catholics were not buried on Sundays. Grandma Miracle's stern gaze did not allow so much as the thought of burying Bernie two days after he died. He had instead to lie in state. Every man from Jessup County to the Tennessee line who had lifted a beer to his lips came to pay his respects. The women and the dries came, too, to make certain that the object of their vilifications had in fact gone to his punishment. All Bernie's family came: brothers, sisters,

130

in-laws, cousins, nieces, nephews. Every moment of every day was filled with people, most of them connected to the Miracle name in some way, either by blood or by law. With every visitor Martha felt judgment like the stab of a maple sword to her heart.

For certainly they knew. If Grandma Miracle knew, if Ossetta knew, if Rosie knew, then the word would have filtered out: Bernie had been a martyr to his wife's philanderings. "She just plain broke his heart."

There was food. Martha would return from the funeral home to find her doorstep littered with Jello salads and jam cakes and fried chicken and noodle casseroles. She filled the refrigerator and the freezer and covered the back porch with food and still it kept coming.

And there were prayers, more prayers even than food. Every night a rosary and the Litany of the Saints, at Grandma Miracle's request the long version, forty-five minutes kneeling. At night Martha soaked her soft Baptist knees in a hot bath and then lay through the night staring at the ceiling, fearing her dreams and praying for sleep. She was afraid to pray for more. She told herself that the God for whom she'd crossed the river was nowhere to be found, but she was afraid to do much looking.

From her dresser their wedding photograph directed accusing glances. She with her eyebrows arched, Bernie with his wink. How could she have known that it was the closest moment they would ever share? That first night she turned it to the wall.

In bed alone (the only time of those long days when she was alone, the time she most needed company) she tried to convince herself that her imagination was running wild, that she exaggerated the suspicion and contempt that she felt from all sides. But imagination proved stronger than will. In brief

131

snatches of uneasy dreams she was pursued by tall, spare figures whose features she never saw, except for the jaw that jutted as sharp and cold and square as a cube of ice.

When morning came she rose to bear alone the burden of her reputation. Talbott was still away, and she was grateful for that. Had he been in town she would have been too tempted to ask for something foolish. She thought of fleeing with him to someplace bigger, more northern, where snow fell from November to April and where she had no name and no husband about to be laid in his grave.

Not that Talbott would agree to such a thing. He would shake his blond head and fear would rise behind his eyes and she'd likely never see him again. But that old perversity rose again, the desire to do something that was not done. Because of it she wanted to leave.

She stayed. At the worst moments, when she caught a stare held a moment too long, or overheard the conversation stage-whispered for her benefit, she made herself stay. At those moments she thought not on her grief, nor on her guilt, but on what she would call hatred, if she dared name it at all. She made herself believe that Bernie had chosen the time and place of his dying; had waited twenty-three years until she broke from his grasp, so as to be able to retaliate in the surest way. In believing that of him, she survived.

*   *   *

Miracle moved through the days as if sleepwalking. Being Catholic, he looked for someone at whom to point the finger, to burden with the blame. He blamed himself for the fight at the Inn, which he saw as the incident which brought on Bernie's heart attack. He blamed his mother for her affair with Talbott, which he saw as the general source of Bernie's troubles. In his own uneasy dreams he blamed the Inn.

132

On the second night after Bernie's death Miracle dreamed that he returned to the Inn. The door banged open in the winter wind. Inside the floor was a mess of broken bottles and bent cans. The room smelled of stale cigarette smoke and flat beer. Behind the bar, in front of the starburst hole of the shattered mirror, stood his father and grandfather and the great-grandfather whom Miracle had never known but whom he knew now instantly, not from the oval portrait above the bar but from his Miracle jaw and bones and flesh and blood.

They ignored him. They walked in a circle, surveying the damage, shaking their heads. From the door Miracle spread his hands and tried to explain: the awful Christmas Eve, Rosamund Uptegrove, Martha and Talbott, it wasn't his fault. His throat was dry as ice. Only a raw croak emerged.

In his waking hours Miracle avoided Martha. If she entered the room he left. If he found himself drawn into a conversation with her and their relatives he excused himself politely. He spoke nothing. He said volumes.

Throughout all, Grandma Miracle hovered at Martha's shoulder like a referee, ushering her through the motions as a mother might lead a bride. In the first days Martha shied from the old woman, wondering what was in this for *her*; when Bernie's mother would seize the moment to draw Martha aside—if she bothered to be so discreet—and speak her mind about Talbott Marquand.

By Saturday evening Martha found herself grateful for Grandma Miracle's presence. An old hand at death, Grandma Miracle insisted on the particulars of ritual. Everything was to be exactly so, down to the choice of mysteries for the Sunday night rosary (Joyful) and the liquor to be served at the wake (beer only until six, then whiskey for the family). She made it perfectly clear where Martha was to be and how she was to act, and though the strain of performance was exhausting,

133

Martha was grateful that it was all so unthinking, like following another's footsteps in heavy snow. She need only lift her
feet and set them down in the old woman's prints.

For the moment Martha followed. Dogging her steps was
the suspicion that when Bernie was irretrievably in the ground,
when the family was back to Louisville and Lexington and the
hills and the hollows, when Martha was left alone with Miracle and Talbott and New Hope and Mount Hermon, the snow
that provided her a trail would melt away, leaving the muddy,
trackless ground of her conscience to cross alone.

As if to bear these thoughts out it snowed, the first snow of
the year, on that Sunday night between Christmas and New
Year's. Sleet pinging against the panes stirred Martha from her
dreams, and she rose to watch it turn from ice to thick snow,
until the porch light cut a white arc through the whirling
flakes. All night it snowed; all night she watched it snow.

The next morning the window sill was buried. In the side
yard the cardinals who made their home in the neighbor's
hackberry tree perched close together on a bare redbud limb,
their feathers ruffled and their bills tucked in their breasts.

The car was snowed in. She and Miracle pulled on boots
and trudged wordlessly the half-mile to the funeral home, the
buckles on Miracle's clumpy black galoshes jingling with
every step.

At the funeral home the undertaker was late. When finally
he arrived he insisted on delaying even more, to let friends and
relatives arrive. The priest started a rosary. No soul would lose
heaven because of negligence on his part.

But almost no one did arrive. The Jackson Highway was
closed north and south. Grandma Miracle made it, and Leo, on
a grader driven by a second cousin once removed who headed
the county road crew. When Martha's parents called, she
begged them to stay home. They were too old, and the tension

134

that came when they and Grandma Miracle occupied the same room was more than Martha could bear. A few other friends who lived nearby and who'd dug out their tractors knelt for the last rosary.

No one came from across the river until at the end of the rosary the door opened. Bradford Uptegrove and Talbott and Big Rosie entered, brought across the bridge in a four-wheel-drive pickup Talbott had commandeered from the construction site.

Martha found herself wrapped in Rosie's arms almost before her eyes had registered the fact that her old friend was there. Cold air washed from the folds of Rosie's fur. Past differences were there—Martha could feel Talbott's presence without seeing his face or hearing him speak—but something larger and older brought Martha and Rosie together: the knowledge that they were women, and that women suffer.

*   *   *

In Mount Hermon and New Hope there are two kinds of weddings: big weddings, where the bride controls her invitation list like a weapon, and only the brashest come uninvited; and small weddings, when the bride is pregnant, or of a different faith than the groom, or perhaps, in Mount Hermon, divorced.

There are only big funerals. For a funeral everyone turns out, rich, poor, timid, brash. All the relations come. After the relations come the elderly who live near the church, who know the deceased only as a face in the post office or by a family resemblance. They come to remind each other that they are still alive, and to mark the shrinking of the community of people who knew life as they knew it. They come to become familiar with death, in the way they might visit a bar the better to know its owner.

135

Whatever their reasons for attending the funeral all expect a wake, with food and (in New Hope) drink and, if the deceased were decently old, perhaps a singing session to follow. Grandma Miracle had planned her oldest son's funeral on that scale. There was the crowd who would come because they knew Bernie or were related to him. Twice again their numbers was the crowd who came to see the crowd, the freeloaders and out-of-office politicians of half a state.

It was an occasion not to be missed, and nearly everybody missed it. Martha prayed fervently throughout the priest's rosary, but she prayed not for Bernie's soul—surely burdened past need with prayers—but that the road crew would not plow the Jackson Highway through to the outside.

Her prayers were answered. The snow was too deep. The undertaker nodded at the priest. Under pretense of looking at the flowers, Martha counted the living: there were twenty-two.

She felt a knobby claw at her elbow. It was Grandma Miracle. "What do you think, child?" she asked.

Martha pretended to give the matter long attention. "The arrangements have been made," she said at last. "The grave is dug. The food is set out at home. I think we should go ahead."

"You're damn right we should go ahead, but not for none of them reasons. This is a Miracle affair and we'll run it exactly how we please. If those no-count children of mine let a little snow stop them from their brother's funeral, why, I say to hell with them, is what I say. Eh?"

Why was it that everybody Martha knew constantly demanded agreement? Grandma Miracle knew what *she* felt—God knows if anybody knew what she felt it was Grandma Miracle—why did she want Martha's opinion? It was the old family need for a unified front: us against them, whoever *they* were. "Yes," Martha sighed, with more resignation than agreement.

"I know how you feel, child. You forget I hadn't always been a Miracle." The claw at Martha's elbow tightened. "Only men ever belong to families, really. They get a name and they grow up with it and they know it will always be theirs, they own it and it owns them. *I* was a Blanchard. That don't mean nothing to you, from across the river. And there's no more of us anyway. There were seven of us, all girls; my daddy tried and tried for a son, he broke hisself and my mamma out trying for a son, and every damned one of us girls. We were a reproach to him, a living mortification. He looked at us and he saw the curse of Job.

"And I looked him back square. That name meant more to me than it ever meant to him because it was mine alone, mine and my sisters', and I watched it disappear and knew that I was the last generation to carry it as my own. I was a Blanchard after I married into the Miracles. We was peaceful folks, Blanchards were, as peaceful as a graveyard under a new moon, and this Miracle crowd seemed like the sons of Sodom to me. I was a Blanchard until the day they brought my husband, Bernie's daddy, up from the river. Then I stood in the Miracle Inn, with all my children around me, Bernie and Leo among 'em, trying to figure out who was going to run the place and if we was going to stay open in the face of those Chicago bootleggers that was cutting people and shooting people and whatnot, and that day I took over the Miracle Inn.

"I expect Bernie never told you I ran the Inn, those years before he was old enough. He was ashamed to have an outsider running the Inn, and a woman at that. I ran it better than him or anybody else before or since, I'll tell you that. Or maybe I should say it ran me. Times was different then, it was harder on a woman. I don't expect you'll have that problem."

Martha stifled a spasm of anger. "You won't see me stepping through that door for love nor money. That's the *Miracle*

137

Inn, in case you hadn't noticed. I leave it to the Miracles. They can chop the place up and use it for firewood, for all I care.''

The claw loosened. ''I know you,'' Grandma said. ''You'll do what's got to be done. That's what every woman does. She sees what's got to be done, and she does it.''

Martha felt the old woman's eyes level with her own, but she kept her own eyes fixed on nothing, somewhere above a floor lamp that diffused light through an inverted saucer of frosted glass. She did not shift her gaze until the old woman yielded her grip.

''That Inn is yours now, and you got a son who's got the name. He's Bernie's son, he's the son with the brains, your brains or mine, I might add, they didn't come of no Miracle that I ever knew, and by rights the Inn is his. I never asked no questions about why one single child and I don't want answers now. You could of had a dozen, it would of been the same by me. But you had one, and he's a man, and he's a Miracle.'' She took Martha's elbow again. ''Let's get in there and get this show on the road before the rest of those no-counts show up and find out what they've missed.''

There were not enough stout men to serve as pallbearers. In the end the undertaker himself lent a hand, to Miracle and Leo. That left Bradford Uptegrove and Talbott Marquand. And so a Baptist and a Yankee helped Bernie Miracle to his grave.

PART TWO

Crossing the River
1968

CHAPTER IX

At the Slate Bed

MARTHA SLEPT a great deal that winter. Hibernation, she called it to Rosie when she called at nine or ten to find Martha asleep; but each morning she woke less rested than the morning before.

Through January she rose with Miracle to fix him breakfast and see him off to the Inn, but he never ate what she fixed and never spoke beyond a few curt words. He left for work and Martha found herself sitting alone with a cooling cup of coffee for company and the long empty day stretching before her like the heart's desert. A morning came when she shut her alarm off bang! and lay eyes open through Miracle's stirrings in the kitchen. She had not risen for him since.

She woke early, stayed in bed late. The terror of rising and the awful responsibility of being alive and alone held her down as surely as any sickness. As long as she lay in bed, the day had not really gotten underway. Some days she lay in bed until noon.

She slept after lunch, dozing in the easy chair whose leather still smelled of Bernie's sweat and aftershave. She buried her nose in the smell, a little penance for her sins. She watched television, hoping to fill the empty hours, but on these clear winter days the reception was terrible. At night she fixed herself a strong drink and sat before the buzzing and flickering images of demonstrations, bombings, big city riots. Behind Strang Knob, at Fort Knox, mock battles raged. With every explosion the television image jumped. She hardly cared. She sat half asleep before the images of another, farther world, until the crash and blare of "The Star-Spangled Banner" sent her to bed, to toss and turn until the coming of another day.

Lying in bed she spent whole mornings avoiding thoughts of Talbott. She had not seen him since the funeral. She had no one to ask of his whereabouts. If Big Rosie knew what he was doing, she was kind enough to keep the knowledge to herself. That left only Ossetta.

Martha had no reason to see Ossetta. Being alone much of the day, Martha had no need for help with her butter or her cleaning. More than once Martha had thought to seek out the old black woman, but always her courage failed her. Ossetta, after all, had been the first to tell Big Rosie about Talbott. Martha could easier imagine stopping the fine ladies of Mount Hermon, the girls she'd gone to school with, married now, to doctors and tobacco farmers and preachers—respectable professions, every one. Martha shuddered at the thought of talking to any of them.

A day came when winter broke, achingly blue and almost warm. Martha lay in bed, staring out her window. From the neighbor's hackberry the cardinals called, *purty, purty, purty*. In midmorning Martha threw back the covers and flung on

142

some clothes. She did not know where to go. She knew only that she was driving herself crazy here.

She walked along the Jackson Highway into town, but the sight of the same stores and street signs and the caution light with its single dead eye was too ordinary and familiar for her to endure. This was the town that Bernie had grown up in, where she had been Miz Miracle for more than twenty years. There was only one place in New Hope that she had ever chosen for herself, and where she could go to escape judging eyes. She went to Assumption Church.

The church was empty. The altars had been stripped bare for cleaning and their Tennessee marble glowed in great splashes of color streaming from the stained glass windows. Martha sat in a hard oak pew, searching for the God who had brought her across the river.

She prayed, first in the memorized prayers of her Catholic Church, then in the person-to-person prayers of her Baptist upbringing. She heard only silence, from without and within.

The windows' dappled light wheeled across the altar in a great arc. Late that afternoon the priest hurried across the nave, dipping briefly in the sideways genuflection of worshipers on the run. Martha fled down the dim aisle to the vestibule.

She paused at the holy water font. In that moment Ossetta entered from the choirloft door.

She wore a navy dress with a small dotted print and a veiled hat Martha had passed on years before. They were alone in the vestibule: the fine-boned, red-haired white woman, smelling of scented soap, and Ossetta, short and stocky and dark as a whiskey barrel, trailing her faint smell of garlic.

Ossetta pretended not to see her. Martha was overcome by rage, against the God she could not find, the husband who had never loved, the son who refused to speak, the lover who had disappeared. She cornered Ossetta under the chalk statue of Saint George, piercing his dragon with a chipped sword.

"Where is he," she demanded.

Ossetta stepped back. "Where is *who*, Miz Miracle."

"You know who. Talbott Marquand."

Ossetta shrugged. "Talbott Marquand. Talbott Marquand. All of a sudden everybody got to know about Talbott Marquand." She turned to the door.

Martha seized her arm. "So where is he."

Ossetta sighed, her breath rustling her veil's thin curtain. "Miz Miracle. I don't know much. What I do know, you don't want to know and don't need to know. You know it already, if you let yourself believe it. But you don't let yourself believe it. That's all right, but if you don't believe yourself, how you going to believe me? Hnnh? So don't axe me questions I can't answer."

"You won't answer."

Ossetta eased herself from Martha's grasp. "That's OK. That's all right, ma'am." She edged from the vestibule.

Martha stepped between her and the door. "Ossetta, why did you tell Rosie Uptegrove?" She'd meant to ask it kindly. It came out as an accusation.

Ossetta stood still, her veil quivering. "Tell her what?"

"You know what. About Talbott. Ossetta, I thought you were my friend."

Ossetta puckered her lips. "Friend! Friend don't have nothing to do with it. I get axed a question straight to my face, I tell the truth, much of it as I knows. Miz Uptegrove axed me did I know if Mr. Marquand came by your place from time to time of a morning, yes or no, and I answered the truth. I don't lie, not for you nor the devil nor Abraham Lincoln." She swept past Martha, her chin upturned. "*Friend*," she muttered, loud enough for Martha to hear. "I don't count no white person as a *friend.*'' She slipped out the side door, leaving Martha alone in the vestibule, cursing and wondering in the dark.

* * *

Suns and moons passed. Miracle discovered that accepting the loss of Bernie to death was easier than accepting the loss of Rosamund to love. Bernie was in his grave. If Miracle needed proof he had only to visit the fresh mound of earth in the Assumption Church graveyard, where proof of Bernie's death was chiseled into pink granite:

FRANCIS BERNARD MIRACLE   1910–1967

With Rosamund, Miracle never knew for certain that things were finished. At Bernie's wake Big Rosie dropped the information that Rosamund was back to her fancy apartment in Nashville—that Talbott had come back a day early from Detroit just to drive her down, and with the weather threatening, no less. If Rosamund got her big break, she never sent word to Miracle. He knew better than to expect word—she'd not written from August to December—but each time a handwritten envelope fell from the Miracle Inn mailbox his heart leapt.

Rosamund sent no letters. Instead Miracle found each day reminders of Bernie. The postman filled his box with an odd mix of letters addressed to Bernie and bills addressed to himself, Michael Miracle, as proprietor of the Miracle Inn. There was the black hole in the mirror behind the white bar, with its starburst of broken silvered shards. Miracle called a Louisville glazier to fix it, but the beveled glass had to be cut to order and weeks went by with him staring into the hole with each sale he rang up.

He was working a cold February morning shift, shoving

beers though the driveup window to the Fort Knox commuters, the day Bradford Uptegrove did not show up for work.

They all came to the Inn looking for him, one at a time. Talbott came first. His blond hair stuck out from beneath his cap and he had mud on his trousers, the first mud Miracle had ever seen on those trousers. For an hour he had been working the backhoe he had trained Bradford to use. Miracle did not take his eyes from the driveup window while Talbott asked about Bradford.

Big Rosie came next, trailing Willie. She dwarfed the door and made the Inn seem a less respectable place than it was. Under her searching Protestant eyes, tobacco stains and peeling walls and the north slant of the pool table all seemed larger than life. Miracle did not tell her that Bradford had talked of going to Nashville. He did not tell her what Bradford had said about LaHoma Dean. After ten minutes she left, trailing doubt as tangible as the scent of Ossetta's asafetida.

Martha called next (on orders, Miracle was sure, of Big Rosie). Since Bernie's death she had not set foot in the Inn, for which Miracle was immensely grateful, especially now. Under her searching blue gaze he would have given way, said something about Bradford's Christmas Eve blabber. On the phone he found it easy to refuse her so much as a word. She hung up angry. Miracle wanted to call back, to tell her that really he knew very little. Then he thought of her waiting for Talbott, those mornings when Miracle was working at the Inn, not a mile away. He hardened his heart. He stayed behind the bar, picking at his sleeves, his nervous hands wandering over his shirt buttons.

The lunch crowd was slow. Talbott had laid off much of the crew until the return of dry weather. Miracle looked up from reading the *Argus* to catch LaHoma Dean standing in the door.

He had hardly seen her since his graduation picnic. She was

146

paler and more moon-faced than ever. She hung at the door, silhouetted against the gray winter light, until he crossed the room to her.

"Where is he, Miracle?" she asked.

Miracle stuck his hands in his pockets and looked out over the bottoms, where the wind whipped corn stubble and broken branches over the ground. "I don't know," he said.

She wore a thin sweater and she wrapped it closer about her, folding her arms. "I promise I won't go chasing after him. I just want someplace where I can send a letter. He'll come back if I send a letter, I know he will."

"I wish I could say, LaHoma Dean," he said. For the first time that day he wished it were true. "He dropped some hints about leaving, he talked about going to California, but you know that."

"I know that. He wouldn't go to California without me."

Miracle wished he himself were so sure. She was not looking at him, but staring out at the tops of the trees along the river, tossing in the wind. "Go home, LaHoma Dean," Miracle said. "This is no place for you to be. You'll catch your death."

"That's the way they did it in the old days."

"You're talking foolishness." Miracle wished she would turn around. Facing her stolid back he felt guilty somehow, as if the weight of one man's sins ought to be borne by them all. He should tell her something, part of him argued, though speaking up would violate every rule of loyalty to his sex and his friend and his Miracle blood. "Maybe he's hunting," he said, hearing the falseness in his voice.

"In February?"

Miracle plunged. "Maybe he's gone to Nashville, or someplace like that. Louisville. Bowling Green. He gets a wild hair."

147

"I know that."

Miracle meant to pat her shoulder, but his pat turned into an awkward little shove. "You go on home," he said. "He'll be back in a week or so."

"You really think so." She did not turn around.

"Sure," Miracle said. "I'll let you know as soon as I see him. If you don't see him first." He stayed outside, watching her struggle against the February wind, across the levee, across the Boatyard Bridge to Mount Hermon.

*　*　*

Martha woke from an afternoon nap to the sound of some-one knocking on the kitchen door. Rosie, she figured, come to grill her again about Bradford. Martha rose, mumbling groggy curses, wrapping a housecoat about her.

It was Talbott Marquand. He stood outside the back door, the jaunty plaid hat perched atop his head, his shoulders hunched against the wind that swept across the valley and through the bare trees. She saw him before he saw her. She considered for a moment, drawing back into her bedroom; then she went to the door.

"I want to see you," he said.

She waved him inside. "Wait here," she said. In her bedroom she put on her clothes slowly. She had no need to hurry. Dressed, she pulled on an old hunting jacket of Bernie's—she'd always worn it for walks in the fields. By the time she noticed what she'd worn, by the time she smelled Bernie's familiar smell, she was in the kitchen, with Talbott. "We'll go for a walk," she said.

"Somebody will see us."

"They won't see anything they haven't already seen. Or imagined."

They climbed the neighbor's barbed wire fence and fol-

148

lowed a cowpath to the river. Devil's walking sticks and the black husks of last summer's blackberry briars grew thick about them. They walked in single file. They did not stop or speak until they reached the river bank.

To the west the mottled flank of Strang Knob rose up, edged with a ragged fringe of bare sumac. Martha sat on the patchy white trunk of a fallen sycamore. Talbott picked up a stick, to scrape at the mud caking the soles of his shoes. "I want you," he said abruptly.

"What about your wife?"

"I'm getting a divorce. That's why I came back early at Christmas. That's why I've come back now. I've been back in Detroit since Christmas, working it all out. She's agreed to it."

"Should I be happy?"

"You should feel however you goddamn please. That's what you're good at, isn't it? Anyway, I didn't get it for you. I got it for me. It's been coming for months. Years. My wife agrees."

"And what about Rosamund Uptegrove?"

Only the faint slap of the water against the slate bed broke the silence that followed, until they both spoke at once. Martha gave way.

"I want her, too. I want you both. I know that sounds bad but it's the truth and you of all people should go easy on me for telling the truth."

Martha thrust her hands into the pockets of her coat. She pulled out spent shotgun casings, scraps of paper, a supply list (in Bernie's illegible scrawl) on a bit of paper sack. This last she stretched flat against the tree's smooth trunk, edging out its wrinkles with her thumbnail. "So what am I to do about this truth. What is Rosamund Uptegrove to do about it."

Talbott shrugged. "That's up to you. You see who I came to first."

"So I should be complimented. Rosamund Uptegrove is younger and prettier, after all. Richer, too, for that matter."

"You love me more. You know that."

She did know that. Her question came before her thoughts. "Then do you love me more?"

He took his hat from his head, turning it around and around in his hands, studying its flybait feather. "There are times when you terrify me," he said.

Below them the river flowed greenly, as cold and sterile as she felt. Talbott took her hand. "It's too soon after—it's been too soon for me to come to see you. It's just that the time seemed right. I've been back and forth to Detroit. I talked it out with my wife. We finally agreed. I had to tell somebody. I told her about you."

"And not about Rosamund Uptegrove."

"No." In his voice she heard the smallest hint of pride. "Only you."

"And was she happy to hear about me?"

Talbott heaved a patient sigh. "Of course she wasn't happy. Any happier than I was to hear about the boyfriend she'd got herself while I was down here. It just seemed right, that we give each other reasons why we wanted a divorce."

"*You* wanted a divorce." Martha folded in neat quarters the little brown paper covered with Bernie's handwriting. "So like you, to plan this all out, with reasons here and reasons there. Every move lined up with a plumb bob."

"What can I say. I'm an engineer."

"Yes. I suppose you are." She stuffed Bernie's list, neatly folded, back into the pocket of his coat. She rose and turned to climb the bank.

Talbott caught at her hand. "Don't leave," he said. For the first time in her life she thought she heard real asking in a man's voice. Or was she hearing, again, what she wanted to hear? Her heels dug into the half-frozen clay. The touch of his soft thick hand brought back other afternoons, that first afternoon in the mountains, when Bernie was off to Louisville and Miracle was at the Inn and Talbott had taken her far away from New Hope.

She looked down at his face, as round and full as a hard-boiled egg. His hat slumped to one side, its feather rustling in the wind. A wisp of hair, palest blond, curled from under its brim.

She started up the bank. "Where are you going?" he asked.

"Back to my house."

He started to speak. She covered his mouth with a gentle hand. "Not a word."

They climbed the bank, slipping and sliding on the half-frozen clay. At the top Martha stopped at a sycamore sapling, waiting for Talbott (in his slick-soled city shoes) to catch up. Inside the pocket of Bernie's hunting jacket she turned over the neat square of paper, pressing its corners into her fingertips.

Talbott slipped. His hand flew out. She grabbed at it. His warm hand closed around her own, that had not touched another's since Grandma Miracle's, the day of the funeral.

He stood at her side, panting, brushing mud from his trousers. She tucked the paper square into a crevice in the sycamore trunk, and took his free hand in her own.

* * *

That night it rained, and the television reception was unusually clear. Sitting before its jump and jabber Martha reflected on the afternoon. She had taken Talbott to her bed to fill the emptiness that was there. He came and went, and she was emptier than before. Was this his fault, or her own?

"Fault, fault. You sound more and more like a Catholic,"

151

she said aloud to the faces on the screen. She sipped the bourbon at her side. She searched for whatever she'd felt only in November, three short months ago, when Talbott and she had risked much more for an afternoon alone.

Where had he been, those months since the funeral? In Detroit, he said. She didn't believe that, any more than Bernie believed her own tales, across September and October and November. She didn't believe it, and still when she touched his hand, when the wind blew his blond hair about, her blood rose and she wanted him hard against her. She wanted only that, nothing more, until that passed.

Then they lay under the wood mosaics, in the same bed where she had turned her back again and again on Bernie. Talbott pressed her for an answer, yes or no.

"Yes or no to what."

Talbott had shrugged, a quick movement of his shoulders so unlike Bernie that it pierced her, a short sharp stab, and for a single moment she hated him for being here; then for a longer, cooler moment, she hated herself: for asking Talbott to her bed; for betraying Bernie, to whom she'd given her word, the man she had married, who had never said, not once, that she was important to him, that he needed her. "Tell me you need me," she said to Talbott: a command, not a question.

"Need?" The bewilderment in Talbott's voice was real. "What has need got to do with it? Either you marry me or you don't." Then she said nothing, until he rose and dressed and left her lying there, alone and shivering and afraid.

Did he need her? Did she need him? Or had they lain there because it was just that time again, like rutting dogs? Need, love—they had never exchanged these words. Much like Bernie and herself, until that day when she'd burned the icing and he'd questioned her love. Now she was here with Talbott, and there was only desire, the same longing that years before had brought her across the river to marry Bernie.

But that was something, she'd felt it strong enough to say yes to Bernie, and then to Talbott, to invite him into her husband's bed. Whatever that was, it had moved her to act, twenty-three years ago and now. Did Talbott feel it in return? He had said, "I want you." To be wanted was something. Was it the same as being loved, as being needed? Surely not.

She knew all that, had known it on that first drive into the mountains, had known it today on the river bank when his blond hair had curled from under the brim of that ridiculous hat. Could she have been such a fool as to fall for a hat?

"Surely not," she said. The pictures on the screen danced on, oblivious.

* * *

At the Inn, Miracle closed that Saturday night's shift early. He counted out the money in the register, pocketed all of it, down to Monday morning's change. He stopped in the doorway where he and LaHoma Dean had talked. He knew where Bradford Uptegrove was, at least for right now. Bradford was a Southern man, broke and on the run. He would go to his family to hide.

Miracle locked the door, turned off the lights. This was his own time to run, to leave this crazy family, and his faithless mother, and this building that sat on his shoulders like original sin. It was his time to leave this town, to declare himself for who he was: Rosamund Uptegrove's suitor, free of his family, shut of his past, with nothing ahead but the wide open spaces of the future.

CHAPTER X

City Lights

As a child, Miracle went to the city exactly once a year, when Martha took him to have his eyes checked. That took a half hour, leaving Martha with a small boy and a full day of errands for herself and half the bridge club. On the third or fourth of these trips Martha discovered that she needn't drag Miracle around. Left with an escalator or an elevator, he entertained himself for hours, riding up and down. In later trips she scheduled Miracle's eye appointment early, with a doctor who kept his office on the top floor of the city's tallest building.

Miracle pretended to blurred vision long after it was clear he would never need glasses. The city drew him back, and the ophthalmologist was his only excuse to go. The idea of a place with traffic, movie houses and neon, people who couldn't tell your family history from the cut of your jaw—all these set the city apart. Things happened there. People who lived there moved as part of a larger world. They made money. lost

154

money, robbed banks, betrayed lovers, swept up broken glass, and built mansions as part of something bigger than themselves. Their smallest gestures took on importance. They were cogs in the larger gears that drove the world of men's affairs.

Miracle's own grandfather had been murdered, dumped in the river in a small, out-of-the-way battle with bootlegging gangs from the city. There were no headlines, no police investigations, no testimonials from outraged politicians. Life went on in its relentless way. Out in New Hope, under the jagged lip of Strang Knob, you could do something small or something big, kiss a man or kill him, it made no difference. It was only in the city that things mattered.

Cruising into Nashville, sitting high on the Greyhound local, Miracle felt that same sense, intensified. Here was a city he'd never seen. He saw it bigger and brighter and cleaner even as the bus negotiated dark and narrow and litter-strewn streets.

Outside the Greyhound station, Miracle bought a clean shirt, a cheap razor, and a doughnut. In the Greyhound bathroom he shaved with cold water. He bought a bunch of yellow daisies wrapped in green florist's paper. He bought himself a map and set off for Rosamund Uptegrove's apartment.

Trash skittered in the February wind. Along the sidewalk the trunks of the few trees were scarred and nicked with slogans and initials. Black men huddled in doorways, scowling when Miracle stopped to ask directions.

Rosamund lived nearby, in a building that looked as if it had not housed a girl of Rosamund's style since before the Civil War. Miracle clutched the flowers in a vise grip and pressed the button. Footsteps approached. He stood back. The door opened. He thrust out his daisies, into the round, stubbled face of Bradford Uptegrove.

155

* * *

"It's been hard, Miracle." Bradford crumbled marijuana onto a paper cigarette, rolled it with one hand, licked the glue. "Want to smoke?"

"No, thanks."

"That's the Catholic in you, Miracle. Come on, give it a try." Miracle shook his head. Bradford lit the joint and poured them both drinks.

Across the afternoon they drank. They talked football and weather and women. With the respect of Southern gentlemen for sensitive topics neither mentioned or asked about LaHoma Dean or Rosamund. The light fell to a late gray February dimness. Sprawled on the couch, Bradford fell asleep.

The daisies drooped yellow heads between the slats of an overturned orange crate. At sunset Miracle heard the door at the end of the hall open. He half-stood and reached for the daisies. The key turned in the lock. He let the daisies lie. She was here, the woman of his dreams.

Rosamund dropped her purse at her feet. "Bradford Uptegrove, are you smoking my goddamn pot again?" She rummaged in the coat closet. Hangers tinkled. "It looks good," she said over her shoulder. "His father's a sound man for Decca. He said they need backups for sure in the next two weeks and he would definitely give me a call." She turned around. Miracle cleared his throat. "Welcome home," he said.

She froze, still as a cat surprised in mid-chase. She eased herself into a Naugahyde easy chair whose arms were patched with gray duct tape. She tapped exactly one cigarette from her pack. Miracle stirred himself to light a match. His hand trembled. Hers did not. She leaned her head back and blew a thin stream of gray smoke into the dark. In the arch of her neck, in

156

the light down edging her cheek, Miracle felt himself losing something he would need to deal sensibly with her and with himself. "So," she said, "what brings you to Nashville?"

"You."

"I was afraid of that."

"You *asked* me to come."

"I'm glad to see you, Miracle, really I am. It's just that it's been a long day and I have to go to work in an hour and I come home to a dump of an apartment with Sleeping Beauty on the sofa bed."

Miracle swallowed hard. This hardly sounded hopeful. But he had come a long way, for one reason. An image flashed across his mind: his mother, striking boldly across the planks of the Miracle Inn to order a beer from Bernie Miracle. He spoke. "I came to—stay with you."

She bent to her purse and pulled out a brush. "It's not your fault. It's just that your timing was a little off." She ran the brush through the underside of her hair. In the twilit room bright trails of static flew from the brush. She tilted her head at Bradford. "Did they send you after him? Or me?"

Was she listening to him? He spoke louder, more insistently. "No. I mean, neither. I came to stay with you." He waited for her to ask him why he'd come, what he meant to do in Nashville, all questions with answers he'd prepared on the long bus ride down. She said nothing. "Where are you working," he said.

"Music City Burger Palace. Graveyard shift." Miracle did not mention the recording contract. "Don't look so morbid," she said. "And whatever you do, don't say anything to Big Rosie and Willie. Nobody hits it big right away. You got to make connections, get squired around, meet the right people. It just takes time, that's all."

"How much time?"

157

"I don't know. Longer for us, Miracle. We got twenty years of catching up with people who grew up knowing how to use a pay telephone." She stubbed her cigarette out. Ashes overflowed, sprinkling at Miracle's feet. "Make yourself at home. I've got to change for work." She stepped into the walk-in closet and shut the door.

The doorbell gargled. Rosamund called from the closet. "Get that, Miracle, would you? I'm not decent."

In the hall it was dark, and he fumbled at the knob. The door stuck, then flew back suddenly in his face. Talbott Marquand held out roses, the largest bundle of flowers Miracle had seen since the fair. Talbott wore a foolish grin. With a shock Miracle recognized a part of himself, fading from the face of the man he most despised. No doubt Bradford Uptegrove had seen the same look on Miracle's own face earlier that day. Only the flowers were different.

Miracle reached for the roses. "Won't you come in?"

"Miracle. What the hell are you doing here?"

"Houseboy. You'll come in? Of course you will."

"Sure, Miracle." Talbott ducked through the door. In his foolish hat, with traces of his grin hanging at the corners of his lips, he looked young, almost kind-hearted. Miracle turned abruptly and walked down the hall. "Wake up, Bradford Uptegrove," he said. "You got company." He knocked on the closet door, opened it a crack and stuck the roses through. "From a secret admirer, Rosamund."

Rosamund stepped out, wearing fishnet stockings and a bow tie and an orange skirt with "Burger Palace" emblazoned on one pocket. She pecked Talbott's cheek. "The roses are lovely, Talbott, and I had no idea both of you were planning to show up or I'd have worked something out but since we're all here we might as well make the best of it. Bradford, roll a joint. Miracle, there's a fifth of Wild Turkey in the freezer and some glasses in the sink. Talbott, have a seat while I put these beautiful roses in something.''

In the kitchen Miracle emptied ice trays while Rosamund arranged flowers in an empty peanut butter jar. ''Since when has he been coming here?'' Miracle hissed.

''Since you started coming here. Can I help it if you both decide to come on the same night? Without saying a word? If you show up by surprise, you can't be surprised by what shows up.''

''He's been here before.''

''If he says that he's just bragging, that's all. Anyway, I'll see him if I want to see him.''

''You won't see him around me.''

''The door's open, I'm not holding you back.'' She ran some water in the jar and started for the living room. Miracle stepped in front of her. ''Miracle!'' she said. ''This is my apartment and I'll see who I want. If you have problems with that you can go home and tend to your bar. Otherwise, sit back and try to be a gentleman. You might learn from the exposure.''

''A gentleman wouldn't keep two women on the string at once.'' The whiskey and the scent from Talbott's roses hit Miracle all at once. He seized Rosamund's shoulders. ''For Christ's sake, Rosamund, he's seeing my *mother*. Doesn't that mean anything to you?''

Rosamund tilted her chin and pursed her lips. ''Why should it mean anything to me? She's *your* mother. And he might still be seeing her—that I don't know—but I can tell you this: he's not seeing her *before* me. And who cares who he's seeing after me? As long as he's seeing me first, he can see half the world later. Probably is. Including your mother.'' She swept past Miracle, roses trembling and trailing faint summer smells.

Miracle poured himself a stiff bourbon and leaned against

159

the sink, contemplating the pattern on the wallpaper. He felt like a rat who'd spent eighteen years learning the ins and outs of a maze, only to emerge into the jaws of a trap. He remembered LaHoma Dean, clutching her sweater about her, hesitating at the door to the Miracle Inn. To cross the river and enter a place she considered hell's vestibule had hardly been less of a journey than his own trip to Nashville; and yet there she'd come.

Thinking about her, shivering in the November wind, Miracle cast aside something he'd grown up with, about what he should do and shouldn't do. He went to the kitchen door and beckoned at Bradford.

He entered, pinching the joint between his thumb and finger. "I thought we sent you after drinks, Miracle."

Miracle plunked ice in two glasses. "You should go back, Bradford." He did not look up. "You owe it to LaHoma Dean."

"The hell you say."

"I'm not saying you should marry her, Bradford. That's up to you and her, and I can think of better matches. But you should go back to figure it out, to let her know something. You owe her that."

Bradford lifted the glass from his hand. "Thanks but no thanks. When I get settled down here—when I have myself some money—I'll think about it then. You just leave that up to me." He poured a dump of whiskey in his glass and fled.

Miracle poured a second drink and followed. He handed it to Talbott and picked up his coat. "Time to go," he said.

"Oh, Miracle, it's late," Rosamund said. "Be a sport. Stick around. You can sleep in my bed, I have to work til six a.m. anyway." She did not rise.

"You can ride back with me," Talbott said. "Really, I'm

160

heading back first thing in the morning. This was just a business jaunt.''

"On Sunday?'' Miracle said. "*I* have the business. I have to be at the Inn by six a.m. tomorrow. Nobody there to hold the fort but me.'' He left, hoping they would call him back. He heard nothing.

He walked to the bus station in a rage of shame and anger. He bought his ticket north with the money he'd taken from the Inn. He'd spent enough for tickets each way, plus a few dollars for daisies and such. Hardly enough missing to matter.

And who would notice anyway? Not Leo, who only checked the register when he needed quick cash for a poker game. Not Martha, who refused to cross the Inn threshold. There was only himself. He boarded the bus north with pain closing like a fist around his heart.

* * *

Miracle was not alone in returning north. Within the week Bradford Uptegrove was back, living at home and submitting to his wedding preparations. From Ossetta, Miracle gleaned that someone had given his whereabouts away to Willie and Big Rosie, who'd hauled him north under threat of revoking his inheritance. Miracle tried to suspect Talbott. When he gave the matter thought Miracle knew the culprit to be Rosamund.

The wedding day came, spitting frozen drizzle. LaHoma Dean wore an off-white dress, a shade shy of virginal. Bradford Uptegrove wore a brand-new double-breasted blazer with gold buttons and wide lapels. Their wedding was small and dismal.

The minister conducted a shotgun ceremony, plain and simple and quiet. LaHoma Dean stood with Bradford before the big glass baptismal tank. Bradford's thin "I do'' might have been the water lapping against its sides. Big Rosie's shoulders heaved as if she were mourning the death of her only son, which, Miracle figured, was exactly how she looked at matters.

Bradford Uptegrove was marrying a girl from the hollers. Tomorrow he was off to boot camp in Texas. In a stormy session with Big Rosie and Willie, he had agreed to marry LaHoma Dean on the condition that he could leave for military service whenever he wanted. Willie agreed. Bradford set himself up to leave the day after his wedding.

The minister smiled, the couple turned to kiss, an embarrassed kiss that carried no joy, no love, no light. Miracle watched, and felt the cold weight of depression sink through his heart and settle somewhere above his spleen.

The service ended. The photographer held the couple at the altar. The first bulb popped. In the flash the image froze in Miracle's mind as if his memory were coated with Kodachrome: Bradford Uptegrove, his lips frozen in a curl, bearing up with the grace of a tortured man facing the firing squad: happy to escape where he'd been, uncertain of where he was heading to. Next to him, LaHoma Dean, quiet and peaceful, her thin cheeks already filled out with the slight thickness of pregnancy, more beautiful than she thought herself to be or would ever be again.

CHAPTER XI

Sweet Dreams

THE HERONS RETURNED with the March rains. Martha heard
their throaty cries at sunrise as she listened to Miracle, bumping around the kitchen before going to the Inn. She had not
heard them since years ago, before she crossed the river, when
she had swum under the Boatyard Bridge and startled the
leggy blue-gray birds from the slate beds.

One day the rain never stopped its steady drumming on the
Miracle Inn roof. That night the creeks came down. The river
spilled its banks. Miracle arrived the next morning to find the
Inn perched atop its little tab of land like Noah's ark on Mount
Ararat. Crows huddled in black clumps in treetops poking
from the flat brown sea. Pigs and chickens, escaped from pens
in the river bottoms, rooted in the Inn's muddy lot. Bits of
upstream lives floated past. Washing machine innards, tractor
tires, broken dolls, animal corpses parked themselves at the
fringe of the levee, until an eddy picked them up and swirled

them on their way downstream, to a riffle or sandbar or to the Gulf of Mexico, a thousand miles south.

Overnight, New Hope became an island. A foot of water covered the Jackson Highway at the Boatyard Bridge. Ten miles north, a creek washed out a culvert. No one could get to work. The town converged on the Inn to get drunk and watch the river rise. By noon every fishing boat in town was docked at the edge of the Miracle Inn parking lot.

Late that afternoon Talbott entered. Across the crowd he caught Miracle's eye and Miracle knew something was wrong, wrong for him, not for Talbott. Talbott crossed to the bar. "A round for the house," he said, and Miracle knew that news about Rosamund rode behind that smile.

The Inn grew quiet, except for shuffling feet and the clink of glass against metal as Miracle poured beers. He covered the top of the white bar with drafts, then moved to the colored bar. When both bars were full Talbott spoke.

Miracle heard though he did not listen, and two minutes later he couldn't have repeated Talbott's words. He heard the men laugh—Talbott must have made a joke—and the cheer from the crowd—that would be Talbott announcing his engagement to Rosamund. Miracle poured drafts, two at a time, until Leo came to spell him for the evening.

Miracle left the Inn to Leo that night. He sat at home before a blank television screen. He was sure his mother had heard the news. She closed her bedroom door and came out only to ask if he wanted supper. He did not.

The silence drove Miracle crazy. He turned on the television and the radio. He poured himself a whiskey, then a second.

It seemed so easy, in principle, to get somebody out of your heart—you just didn't think on them. But his Pickett heart had a mind of its own, traveling worlds apart from his head's

164

wishes and demands and desires. And his heart's mind, his more powerful mind, was fixed on Rosamund Uptegrove.

Miracle considered this through his second drink. At the Inn Talbott had said that Rosamund was back in town, for the formal announcement of her engagement. Fortified by whiskey, led by perversity, Miracle rose at midnight, drove to the Inn, and parked in the middle of the Jackson Highway.

The blue hum of the parking lot's mercury light overlaid the silence. In the middle of the river Miracle saw the black webbing of the Boatyard Bridge against the paler black of the sky. He untied Leo's boat. He fit the oars in the locks and rowed.

He landed a mile downriver from Mount Hermon, in a feed lot empty of cattle but knee deep in soggy manure. He struggled to a tiny island of solid earth at the base of a fence post. The bourbon he'd drunk had long worn off. The muck slurped at his boots. He clung to the post and measured the distance to firm land: twenty yards or more.

This, Miracle thought, is what they call love.

He fought his way through a mile of muddy fields and barbed wire fences to Mount Hermon. At the Uptegroves, Rosamund opened her window at his first knock. She raised a finger to her lips. "You can come through the back door," she said. "But take off those shoes. God, Miracle, you think you'd been wallowing in a pigpen."

Inside, she stood him in the center of her room. "Don't move, and don't sit down, whatever you do. I'll be back in a second."

In his visits to the Uptegroves, Miracle had never been in Rosamund's room. It was large, patterned with roses. Scattered among the roses were signed photos of Nashville stars, a regular Saturday night lineup at the Grand Ol' Opry. Loretta

Lynn, Tammy Wynette, even Minnie Pearl, her hat covered by a corner of a photo of the great Patsy Cline edged with a strip of black ribbon.

"You smell like a feed lot," Rosamund said from the door. "Take those things off and put this on." She handed him a bathrobe trailing the faint smell of men's cologne.

She wore a long robe, edged with roses and cinched at her waist, the same sort of high-waisted, low-cut gown that caught his breath last summer at the county fair. It caught his breath now. "So what took you so long," she said.

Miracle's heart rose; this sounded promising. "How was I to know you wanted to see me. You didn't exactly throw out the welcome mat in Nashville. You disappeared after Bradford's wedding. You never wrote. There was Talbott hanging around—" In the struggle to get where he was, Miracle had forgotten Talbott's announcement of the engagement. The suspicion occurred to him, as unmistakable as the scent of cologne about his bathrobe, that Rosamund was used to receiving guests through her bedroom window.

"What does it matter what I think," Rosamund said smoothly. "If you wanted to come, you should have come."

Miracle knew this argument had flaws at the same time he couldn't put his finger on them. Rosamund gave him no time. "What are you waiting for? Get out of those pants." She sat on her bed. "Come on, climb in. You're freezing."

"But what about Talbott! You're engaged! To be married!"

"So I am. That doesn't change the fact that you're freezing. Climb in." She lay back, pulled the covers into a high tent with one hand, pointed under them with the other.

For a moment Miracle hesitated, staring at the floor, overwhelmed by conscience and duty and honor and religion. Then he raised his eyes and looked, and was lost.

They made love. Rosamund gave him condoms she pulled

from a music box covered with roses. With Rosamund's breasts round and full in his hand, Miracle gave himself over to sex.

She was sweet and soft and full. She took him like he'd not been taken, even in his dreams, in those holy, lonely nights under the north pilings. She touched him here and there until he thought only of wanting her, wanting to be inside her. Then he was inside her, and his mind went away and he rode her hard, hard as a stallion fucking a first-time mare in the hot hard light of the stock pen, so hard some small part of him feared he was hurting her, and he rode her harder still, emptying his jealousy and anger and lust and fear into her body. When it was over he fell back, tears rolling from his eyes. He hid his face in her rose-covered quilt. Ah, yes, he thought. This is what they call love.

They lay together, Miracle with his arm about her shoulders as calmly and naturally as if he had slept with Rosamund for the year since his graduation. Rosamund crooked one arm behind her neck. "Open that nightstand drawer and hand me that little blue box." From the box she pulled some tissues and an array of bottles with pointed caps. She smoothed the quilt between them and spread a thick *Cosmopolitan* flat. She arranged the bottles in a semicircle and took the top from one. The heady smell of acetone filled Miracle's head. With exquisite care she spread the fingers of her left hand, brushing each red-painted nail with polish remover. In the calmness his questions returned. He stared at the ceiling, spent and afraid, stumbling about for a way to begin. Rosamund saved him the trouble.

"Miracle, I'm marrying Talbott Marquand for a lot of different reasons, but only one counts. He can get me to Nashville. He doesn't have the connections he said he did, but he's got the money, Big Rosie has that one checked out. He'll get me out from under her thumb, at least. After that, *I'll* make the connections. I'm good at that. I can have a career with him. No screaming babies, no dirty diapers. Marrying Talbott Marquand kills so many birds with one stone I feel like I'm dovehunting a baited field.''

''Is that what getting married is about?''

Rosamund shrugged. ''We'll get divorced if it gets too messy. I'll write a song about it.''

Miracle's face gave his heart away. ''Oh, Miracle, don't look so mortified,'' Rosamund said. ''You're as bad as Mamma. She acts like singing in Nashville is just a stage I'll grow out of as soon as I find my Talbott Marquand to *fuck* it out of me. Or buy it out of me, one. Really! You'd think they never had a dream in their life, none of 'em, except for living in a new brick house with four white columns and a little chalk darky at the end of the drive.''

''Rosamund, everybody has dreams. Lots of them.'' Miracle's words came tumbling from his lips, jarred loose by the sharp slap of Rosamund's attack. ''Some people keep their dreams a little close to the chest. But everybody dreams about *something*.''

Rosamund rolled her eyes. ''Miracle, it's the Catholic mentality. You're cursed with it,'' she said patiently. ''Complicated, in your case and your mother's, by the Pickett heart.''

Miracle sat up. ''Now what the hell does *that* mean?''

''Head in the clouds. Crazy ideas. Marrying for love. People with circles floating over their heads.''

''Halos.''

''Whatever. Everybody *I* grew up with wants a nice, solid brick house with four white columns.''

''That's not true. I know people from Mount Hermon who grew up with dreams as crazy as anybody's.''

''Such as?''

168

Miracle shifted his weight away from Rosamund, to stare at the rose-patterned wallpaper. "Such as my mother."

Rosamund screwed the top on the acetone. "My point *exactly*." She took up a violet tissue and stripped each nail of its scarlet sheath. "Your mother wanted love. She left everything she knew behind for that. Took off like a bat out of hell. And look what happened to her."

"It doesn't matter what happened to her," Miracle said. "You still got to do it. It's something you got to do, and you do it."

"*You* do it."

"It's the love that matters. It's natural to love something you can't hold in one place and measure with a ruler."

"So what do you love?"

"You," Miracle said.

"I was afraid you'd say that." Rosamund twisted open a bottle of rose-colored polish. With perfect steadiness she touched the brush to each clean fingernail. Then she lay back, fanning her freshly-painted nails back and forth. "I care about you, Miracle. You can't help caring about somebody you catch jacking off under the Boatyard Bridge, the first time you meet them. I like you a lot. But that won't get me to Nashville." Miracle dropped his head to the sheets. "Oh, come on, Miracle, I want to be a star. *You* understand what it means to want something so bad you'll do anything for it."

"Yes," Miracle said. "Oh, yes."

"Then make it easy for me, OK? Shake my hand. Blow me a kiss. Wish me luck. Buy my records." She leaned across the bottles to kiss him, holding her still-glistening nails high above his head.

The window framed a pale gray sheet of sky, and Miracle realized that it was dawn, that he had spent the night, for the first time in his life, in a woman's bed. He sat up abruptly,

169

swinging his legs over the side of the bed. He felt tears returning. Rosamund Uptegrove was the last person he wanted to see him cry.

"Where are you off to?" she asked.

"I got to get out of here before Willie Uptegrove skins my hide for rolling in the hay with his *engaged* daughter. Not that Willie would care about anything so idealistic."

"Oh, Miracle, you're mad. That's another thing about Catholics, you're so damned touchy."

Miracle struggled into his pants. Slivers of mud showered onto the carpet. He shoved his arms into his sweater and it fought back.

"We're both dreamers. Can't you see that?" Rosamund said. "You and me. *And* your mother. All three of us. It's just that what I'm after is *real*. Nashville is real. Money is real. You and your mother—you're after love. And love is not real. Only a class 'A' dreamer would row across the river in a March flood for love. That's just you, and your mother. You'd never catch me doing that for love. For a recording session, maybe. Not for love."

"Yeah, well, you won't catch me at it in the near future," Miracle said. "I'll see you at the wedding. If I'm invited." Before she could answer he tiptoed from the room.

Across the muddy fields he raged at Talbott, at Nashville, at Rosamund, at himself. Last summer there had been a river, barely a creek, separating him from Rosamund. Now there was a flood, a mile-wide muddy mess of uprooted hopes and broken dreams.

Slogging through the cold water, Miracle stoked his heart on thoughts of revenge. Its promise gave fire to his blood. He would tell Talbott of this night, spent with his fiancée, at her invitation. If that made Talbott break the engagement, Miracle couldn't care less. That was Talbott's affair. Miracle wanted

170

only to sow, as thickly as possible, the seeds of unhappiness that filled his heart.

* * *

Earlier that night, Martha had heard Miracle when he set out south on the Jackson Highway. With the understanding of one who had crossed the river herself she knew where he was going and guessed how he would get there. She thought of stopping him, because it was dangerous and because she did not consider Rosamund Uptegrove worth the risk of life, limb, and peace of mind.

She raised her hands over her head. "Let him go," she said. Since Bernie had died she talked to herself, sitting at her bureau mirror, under the gaze of the twin wood mosaics of Jesus and Mary of the Seven Sorrows. "Talbott Marquand was hardly worth risking life and limb for. And Bernie Miracle. And here you are." She composed her hands in her lap.

The night that followed was the longest of her memory, longer than setting watch while Bernie lay in the funeral home, longer than the night so many years before, when in the same bed and under the same pair of Sacred Hearts bleeding drops of cherry blood, she had turned her back on Bernie Miracle.

From the point of view of nearly everybody she knew, she had betrayed both sides of the river. In Mount Hermon they thought she had left her family and religion to marry a heathen who made his living trafficking in sin. In New Hope they thought of her as an outsider with loose morals and liberal ideas that no doubt had their source in divorce or some equally radical Baptist notion.

"You got to run with the foxes or run with the hounds," Ossetta had told her once, before Miracle was born. Martha had been run by them both and now she felt cornered, treed with no strength to run and no place to go if she'd been able.

171

Across that white night she sank down. She moved to the armchair, Bernie's rocker, and breathed Bernie's faint and fading smells from its antimacassar. She sank to the depths alone, so far down that some part of her feared for her return. She had been certain that for her there was no defeat. Now she was defeated.

Down into the wreck; many wrecks, really, piled atop each other like the layers of fires and flint and bones left by the Indians in the limestone crevices of Strang Knob. Her marriage to Bernie; the child born to neither side but somewhere in between, who looked more and more as if he would be content to stay in this town; and worst of all, Talbott Marquand, who had pressed her for an answer that she had refused to give. Strewn through these wrecks were her hopes for her new religion, for the incense and candles and mystery of the Church.

Back in the bedroom, she stared at the wood mosaics. They had hung there since before she moved into the house. Grandma Miracle had hung them there, because every bedroom should have its Jesus and Mary, and because she hadn't trusted this new, Baptist bride to do her job. They were terrible faces. Looked at closely, something in the grain of the wood, tortured around the eyes, gave forth the pain hidden behind the beatific smiles.

Looking at them she touched bottom, in a different, deeper place than after Bernie's death. Then the bottom she had touched was as soft as Knobs Fork clay in a spring flood. She had lain there wallowing in regrets and recriminations until now. Sitting under these suffering gazes she found her strength, the hard, bedrock place inside herself, the place that she'd leapt from when she crossed the river that first time, and when she'd walked into a Catholic church, and when she'd fought with Bernie to have their single child and no more.

172

Once she had loved being alive. She loved being wild, she took pride in the rumors and the sideways glances and the knowing that things were changing, even here, because of her. For twenty years that pride had shamed her, when she dared face it at all. Now, sitting below the wood mosaics, she embraced it, as part of who she was.

She rose and put on a coat. Her own coat, not Bernie's, she made sure of that, with a mental note to call the Saint Vincent de Paul Society and give them everything that ever belonged to her dead husband. In the first gray light of dawn she set out in search of Talbott.

She did not look long. He was at the Inn, alone at the bar. She entered and shut the door softly. She crossed the room and tapped him on the shoulder. He turned. "You son of a bitch," she said.

For a moment he spread his hands—asking for help? Then he stuffed his hands in his pockets, as if he'd been caught at some shameful act. "I was hoping I'd see you, Martha. We need to go somewhere and talk."

"Talk." She waved at the empty room. "We can talk here, if that's what you want."

He put his hand over her mouth. "Leo is here, passed out in the back room. We might wake him up."

"I'm not afraid. What have I got to be afraid of? Go ahead, talk. You got an audience."

Talbott turned to his beer. She counted, one, two, three . . . "I loved you," he said finally.

He said it, she'd known he would, now that it was safe to say it, now that he was home free. "Love," she said bitterly. "That word. What right do we have to it, either of us." His hands searched for hers; she drew them away. "No, you didn't love me, at least not according to anything I'd call love. But I didn't love you either. You were going somewhere you needed

173

to go. I was a handy way to get there. If that sounds terrible that's OK, because it's a true fact. I know it's true because the same thing is true for me.''

"No," Talbott said. "For whatever it's worth, no. I understand what you're saying. It's what all those women in New Hope are saying. Love—you're right, it's the wrong word. But when I think back on those mornings, when I told everybody down here I was going to buy some shit at Mallory's and I got in the car and I prayed that you'd be at home alone and sometimes I got lucky and you were, I think back on that and I think about putting a name to it, some word to pin on it, and I don't know of any other word to use. You got a better word, I'm listening.''

She heard some sense in what he was saying, and even as she heard it she knew that the time would come when she'd be able to acknowledge that sense. But that time was not now, not here, in the place that once had been Bernie and that now was her, herself and her only son. "Maybe there is no word," she said. "But there's trusting somebody and treating them with decency, there's saying no sometimes to yourself because that way you can say yes to somebody else. There's needing somebody—saying to somebody, once in a while, 'I need help. I need *you*.' That's what I'd call love. Is that what you felt on those mornings when you were hellfire to come out to the house?" Her voice rose. "Is that what you felt when you took off to Nashville?''

Twenty-four hours, twenty-three years of maintaining and suddenly she was overwhelmed. She'd felt this coming when she put on her coat, when she left the house, but she trusted in herself, in the strength of Martha Pickett, to ward it off, to keep things under control. Now she saw Leo Miracle in the storeroom door, his jaw slack as a scarecrow's, and in seeing him she broke. Take it all in, she thought, for a long delirious

174

second before she reeled back her hand and slapped Talbott's ruddy fair cheek as hard as she could, so hard that his hat, that funny, dumpy hat, flew from his head to land on the bartop. Then she turned and left, stepping carefully across the uneven floor, shutting the door as softly as when she'd first come in.

Outside, the river had begun to fall. Empty milk cartons and a single forlorn glove marked the high water line. Farther out a heron waded among the stubble of last summer's corn, a pale blue tear against the muddy brown backwash. To the south, fighting the current that surged around the bridge pilings, she saw Miracle rowing a dull, battered boat.

He moved forward a few feet. The current spun the boat around and tangled it in a mass of matted snags and branches and trash. He stood halfway, his hands on his hips, surveying the mess that entangled the boat. He cursed; she saw his head jerk in angry spasms.

From where she stood, atop the Inn's dry tab of land, he looked so fragile against the flood. At any moment a surge of current might tip the boat and throw him into the water, smashing his head against the pilings. "Miracle, sit down!" she shouted. With the wind against her words she was certain he did not hear.

As if on cue he sat. He took an oar from its lock and pushed at the tangled limbs. Suddenly he drifted free, turning and bobbing in the current, and then he was in calm backwater, growing larger as he rowed closer, until she could see his familiar square chin, Bernie's chin, and that Pickett red hair, her own hair.

The boat crunched into the gravel of the parking lot. He turned around. "I don't know where you've been to get looking like you are, but I won't believe any story you could make up so don't bother," Martha said. "Get yourself home and get changed and get back down here. You've got a

175

business to run, and I'm here to help you do it." She meant to sound like a conspirator. Instead she sounded as if she really cared that his clothes were muddy and that he was late to work.

"Yes, *ma'am*," he said.

She quailed before the razor's edge in his voice. "Oh, Miracle," she said, but he was tugging the boat ashore and Leo was yelling at them from the lot and Talbott was tearing out of the drive in his red Mustang.

Too much to say, and so she said nothing. How could she expect her son to forgive her? How could they talk, with Leo shouting in their ears? The moment slipped from her as surely as time. Martha trudged home, leaving Miracle cursing and struggling at the water's edge.

CHAPTER XII

Hunting Snipe

THE RIVER DROPPED. Before the week was out Talbott was back on the new bridge. Standing at the Inn's window, Miracle watched him pace the length of the bridge's white concrete, shouting, arguing, pointing. Only the last smooth concrete and asphalt skin remained to be laid.

A morning came when Miracle rose earlier than usual. Instead of walking to the Inn, he turned onto the levee that Talbott and his crew had constructed for the new bridge. He found Talbott among the machinery, sipping coffee from a styrofoam cup. "I want to take you for a walk," Miracle said.

"I've got business to attend to, Miracle," Talbott said.

"So do I. They'll get along without us. You've left your business alone plenty of mornings. I know that and I know where you went when you left. You went there on and off since September, as far as I can tell, every morning you could

177

get free that my father was at the Inn. You can give me a little time in exchange.''

''Miracle, you don't just go off and leave—''

''She's my mother, Talbott Marquand, and Rosamund Uptegrove was my girlfriend.''

''I have to wonder what Rosamund would say to that.''

''I know the answer to that. I can give it to you here, in front of anybody that shows up. Or you can come along.'' Miracle turned around without waiting. Talbott crumpled his cup into a wad, tossed it behind a bulldozer and followed.

Across the fields Miracle heard the sweet tolling of the morning Angelus. He should be at the Inn by now. He could name the men already lined up at the driveup window.

He climbed Strang Knob, pushing though the brown stubble of last year's teasel and sagebrush. At his back he heard Talbott's labored breathing. Miracle pressed on, climbing harder and faster.

''You're responsible for a business,'' Bernie said at his ear. ''People depend on you. People find out they can't depend on you, they go somewhere else. The Inn has been here longer than any place else because people know they can depend on us. And I give it over to you because I know I can depend on you.'' Miracle climbed on.

At the cliff edge Miracle paused to let Talbott catch up. Below, Miracle picked out the red tiled roof of Assumption Church, and to the south the white clapboard siding and steeple of the Mount Hermon Baptist Church, poking from the square. Between the towns the river twisted and turned like an emerald snake. In the river bottoms the Inn sat alone, a tiny black cube on a tab of earth projecting from the levee. A line of trucks and cars wound from its lot.

''They'll go to the Inn and have a drink on us, whether they know it or not,'' Bernie said at his ear. "Maybe they'll get to where they don't feel so bad about themselves and the world."

Miracle turned his back on the Inn. He crossed the spine of the ridge to a limestone outcropping on its western face. Talbott followed.

Beyond the western foot of Strang Knob, on the firing ranges of Fort Knox, the grayness began, a vastness of burned and blackened tree stumps. The river disappeared green behind a ridge and emerged to wind gray and brown through scarred fields. Older craters, left by bombs, had eroded to brown holes, but red clay bled forth from new gashes.

Talbott sat on a stump, panting. "I hope this is worth it,'' he said. "I don't go for morning walks for recreation."

Miracle wheeled around then, to face Talbott head on. "Why have you used us like you have? First my mother, then Rosamund Uptegrove. Why can't you leave us alone? When I finally figured out what you were up to I didn't believe it. Partly I didn't believe it because I didn't want to believe it. Mostly I didn't believe it because it didn't make sense. Here we are out in the middle of nowhere and this guy comes in with a little bit of money and a red car and screws up our lives. And what the hell for? I thought about it until finally I couldn't think of any reason for it at all except that you saw two more women to add to the list. Just nothing but meanness, pure and simple."

"Meanness," Talbott said. "Well."

A jet streaked overhead, so low its roar drowned his voice. Talbott removed his hat, the dented plaid hat with the feather tucked in its brim. He fanned his flushed cheeks.

The jet faded to the south. "I told them," Talbott said. "I told them both early on that I was married, that I had a wife."

"So that makes it all right."

179

"No. There's no way to make it all right." Talbott stood, planted his feet, crossed his arms: he might be lecturing a tardy worker. "Now you listen to me. You think about how things were. Just my taking this job, just my showing up changed everything, here and back in Detroit. I went back there after my first weeks down here and I ran into a whole lot of choices. I could try to fix my marriage up, and if I got lucky I might get it back to the mess it was in before I left to come south. I could stand back and do nothing but help my wife pack her bags. Or I could figure out what I wanted and come back here and try to get it. I came back from that trip north and I asked your mother to go for a drive to the mountains. And she said yes, because she wanted to go."

"Then why didn't you finish it out!" Miracle cried. "My father's dead now, you could have asked her to marry you. But no, you had to go after Rosamund Uptegrove."

Talbott picked at the feather in his hat. "Rosamund Uptegrove I understand. That's why I proposed to her. It's why she said yes. This time I know what I'm doing. With my wife, with your mother—I was never sure. With Rosamund, I can say I'm sure about something. We'll get married, build a house, have a kid or two, she'll settle down. We'll fit together just fine."

"What about her going to Nashville?"

Talbott laughed, something like a hoot. "She just *thinks* she wants to go to Nashville. She doesn't know what she wants. That's what I can do for her—help her figure out what she really wants, not just what she *thinks* she wants. Rosamund needs a man, needs *me*. I don't expect you know this, but I asked your mother to marry me. Every time I asked—"

"A lot of asking for somebody who's spent two of the last three months in Detroit," Miracle said scornfully.

"—every time I asked she said no. She had these conditions. Imagine you ask a woman to get married and she says, 'Only if you need me.' Not that I wanted her, not even that I loved her, but that I need her. That *I* need *her*.'' Talbott beat his hat against his leg, until the feather came loose and flew towards the lip of the cliff. ''That's when I headed for the door.''

The draft that rose up the Strang Knob cliff carried the feather up, until it tangled itself in the limbs of a dogwood just threatening to break into bloom. Miracle watched the feather thrashing in the branches—it was stuck fast. He thought of himself with Rosamund, the last time he'd seen her. His fingers bent slightly, recollecting the curve of her breasts, how round and full each had rested in his cupped palm; all the while she was contemplating which nail polish would best match the next morning's blouse. Miracle saw her touching liquid pink to each nail's pale crescent, and in that same moment the barn door of things, that had been staring him full in the face: the worst thing Miracle could do to Talbott was to keep his own mouth shut, to leave Talbott to figure Rosamund out on his own. And he would, soon enough—he wasn't *that* dumb, and anyway, how dumb could you stay with Rosamund Uptegrove as a teacher? Down the pike—two years? three years? Long enough for the ink to dry on the papers, long enough for the paint to dry on the columns of the new brick house; long enough for Rosamund to figure out the next step and go for it.

Miracle stepped over to the dogwood, where the feather kicked and struggled like some live thing trapped. He freed it gently, gave it to Talbott. ''You never deserved my mother in the first place,'' he said.

''And I didn't get her either. So now we're all happy, right?''

Miracle turned and walked away. He stumbled blindly through the undergrowth, catbriar and the canes of last sum-

mer's blackberries tearing at his jeans. Love, that was easy.
He'd said it himself without much trouble in the saying, had
heard it often enough on television, on the radio, had read it in
the romance novels his Grandmother Pickett stole from the
bookmobile and hid at the Miracle house once she'd finished
their reading. But need? That was another place altogether.
Miracle had to admit it—he'd understood Talbott there. Miracle tried to imagine himself saying to Rosamund Uptegrove, to
anybody, "I need you." No luck. Need was for the weak. A
man didn't need somebody unless he was weak, unless he was
sick or laid up with a broken leg, or crazy maybe. And Miracle
was a man, from strong stock, Miracle stock, who had the
good sense to hold his tongue when that was the best and worst
thing he could do.

The problem was, he needed somebody right now. He sure
could use a body right now. Would he ever be able to say that
to another person, woman or man?

Miracle walked a ways, how far he couldn't say and didn't
care, until he tripped over a root and fell flat. The ragged edge
of Strang Knob rose to greet him like an old lover. He lay
against it, scratched and sore, above the bombs and flares of
the mock war to the west.

* * *

Martha was sleeping when Leo called. She stumbled to the
phone. She tried to recall if she'd heard Miracle leave for the
Inn.

That was exactly what Leo wanted to know. Estill Mallory
had called Leo from the store. For the first time in anybody's
memory the Inn was not open for the Louisville commuters.
How could a working man be expected to drive an hour and a
half each way without a six-pack of beer? Leo wanted to
know, and how in the hell was *he* supposed to do something

182

about it, with a cow about to calf and Dolores gone to the county seat to bowl, for Christ's sake? In the middle of his tirade, Martha gently replaced the receiver. She dressed and drove to the Inn.

The little tab of land surrounding the Inn was packed with knots of men standing and cursing in clouds of white vapor. Martha parked and weaved through the cars, meeting no one's eyes. Inside, she flipped up the driveup window. "Sorry for the delay," she called into the lot. "Miracle's sick. Leo is busy. What can I do for you?"

Silence. Several men (children of the men who had walked out that first night Martha had walked into the Miracle Inn and ordered a beer) climbed in their cars and spun out of the lot. Among the rest there were sheepish faces and mumbled jokes, but they lined up. A gentleman proved his mettle in just this sort of trying situation. They were not to be caught with their manners down. More than one doffed his cap and squeezed her hand and told her how sorry he was to hear of Bernie's death, now Miracle was sick, it never rained but it poured, my wife put in so much canned okra it's running out our goddamned beg your pardon ears, I could drop it down to Miracle, he's a good boy and the pride of his family, you're lucky to have him thank you very *much*. Twenty of these speeches and Martha was on the verge of slamming the driveup window on some well-meaning hand.

Then they were gone, in the way of the Inn's schedule. She was alone. She wiped the bar and dusted the bottles. The morning stretched on. Squares of light turned across the floor and the north-slanting pool table. Still no one came.

Martha delighted in the work. She emptied the coolers and wiped them out. She took the bottles from in front of the unbroken mirror and washed it down. Across that morning she worked, without thought of Miracle or Bernie or Talbott, until

Leo arrived, just before the noontime rush. "What the hell's going on here?" he said.

Martha shifted a case of bottles to the cooler. "Open your eyes, Leo, you'd think you grew up with those blind fish in Mammoth Cave. It's dinner time at the Inn. Where have you been?"

"Some of us have a farm to attend to."

"And some of us have a business. We can thank God there's enough to keep us all working hard. Would you fetch another case from the stockroom?"

Leo was at the door to the stockroom before he caught himself. "I mean, what are *you* doing here, Martha Pickett? Alone? Tending bar like some hoptown floozy. And where's Miracle?"

"He's sick. A body has a right to get sick every now and then."

"Sick, hell. Bernie didn't get sick in fifty-seven years."

"And look what happened to him. They're different persons, or hadn't you noticed? Bernie is dead. Miracle is alive. Leo, we'll have some real live customers in about ten seconds and I want to be ready for them. Either get with it or kindly remove yourself to the other side of the bar."

Leo straddled the narrow aisle behind the bar. "You forget, Martha Pickett, who *is* in this family and who is *not*. I'll be damned if I'll let a woman—"

"Haven't you got a farm to attend to."

"This is Miracle business. Somebody from the family's got to be here."

"Somebody from the family *is* here, Leo, or at least the side of it that has any gumption. You're welcome to stay, if you keep out of the way."

Leo spread his bony hands in a wide fan, as if studying his fingernails for dirt. "OK," he said. "But don't think you've heard the last of this. Not from the Miracles." He stomped out.

Martha served the lunch crowd, cleaned up, was alone again. She moved to the window then, watching the construction crew across the old levee, as they paved over the turnabout where a few months earlier she had sat watching for Talbott and dreading Bernie's appearance at this same window.

She puzzled on how it was she got herself into such messes. *Her* parents built a house (not too large), bore children (not too many), feared God (not too much), and set out to live as prosperously as possible within the bounds of good taste and the Baptist Church. *She* traveled from one extreme to the next. Her parents' lives stretched out before and behind them like Kansas, with only a dip here and a rise there to accommodate the traumas—death, birth, marriage, taxes—that no one could avoid. Her own life mapped out like Jessup County itself, full of sharp ups and downs and craggy limestone cliffs and sudden sinkholes where springs gushed forth, where the earth trembled endlessly from the mock battles fought just over the next hill.

She worked through that day, until Leo arrived for the evening shift. She greeted him pleasantly. He grunted a response.

At home she found Miracle asleep in Bernie's chair, his hair matted and his jeans covered with sticktights and cockleburrs. She covered him with a quilt and retired to a sound and dreamless sleep.

She found him there the next morning, curled into a ball, the quilt tossed to one side. She left him sleeping. The Inn was hers, too, after all, Grandma Miracle said as much. It was Martha Pickett's turn to run it now. She could run it now, better than the best.

CHAPTER XIII

Blood Talk

SHE FACED THEM ALL. When she had to, she faced them down.

The next morning, Miracle rose with Martha. She ordered him back to bed. She would take the morning shift; he could come at noon. Miracle gave her a long look of disbelief, then he shrugged and returned to his room.

After twenty-three years boldness did not come easy to Martha Pickett Miracle. Standing at the driveup window on the fourth or fifth morning, she could no longer offer Miracle's illness as an excuse. Her stomach roiled; her palms grew icy. She welcomed them all, gave some a friendly smile, others a steely gaze.

Mornings at the Inn became part of her life. The place had its way of working into the blood, and Martha welcomed it with an open heart. The talk, and the traffic; being part of the town; doing something she was not supposed to do, going places she had never been; she welcomed these. Some of the

186

men refused to buy from a woman and stayed away. Most came every morning, though there were complaints and jokes from outside the window.

Martha took care to give them full chance to speak their doubts. She took that as her penance, for the years with Bernie when speaking had been possible and she had not spoken. Working at the Inn, where Bernie had spent most of his waking hours, she felt the old wounds begin to heal.

The work was not a pleasure. It was dull, and there were always men who felt it their duty to remind her of her place and how she'd come by it. They did it casually and with a politeness due a widow and a woman. They conjured Bernie's memory, referring in sly jokes to her affair with Talbott, or to the ways (always better) that Bernie had run the Inn.

Martha listened and held her tongue. Working at the Inn she cleansed herself of sins, her own and Bernie's, twenty years in the making.

She was at the Inn reorganizing the shelves when a work crew arrived from Louisville unannounced, to install the new, custom-cut beveled mirror, replacing the mirror broken in the Christmas Eve brawl.

Leo arrived for his dinnertime beer as the men were wrestling the crated mirror from their van. With a heavy scowl he stood about, eyeing the crew and the mirror from different angles. "A sorry looking crowd, if I do say so myself," he said. "Two niggers, which means that whoever's hiring in that company is hiring cheap. And if the white guy was any good at what he did he wouldn't work with niggers. You wait and see."

Martha was handing change through the driveup window when she heard a workman grunt. Leo cursed. She whirled around to find Leo already through the hinged flap in the bar. One corner of the mirror rested on the bartop, where it had dug a scratch, a long sliver of white across the dark mahogany. Leo was lecturing one of the workers, a short squat man who might have been one of Ossetta's long-removed sons. "Leo," Martha called out sharply. "I asked you to stay out of the way."

"He was *dropping* it."

"Then he would have paid for it, or his company. Leo, *leave*. Go back to the farm. *Please*."

He gave her a look to clabber milk. "I'll go, Miss Priss. But I'll be back."

Martha watched him storm through the door. From the rear he might have been Bernie, the same narrow shoulders and slightly bow-legged Miracle strut, until he slammed the door, something Bernie, with his slow anger, would never have done.

Martha and the workmen were washing the mirror of bits of putty and fingerprints when Leo returned. The first person Martha saw reflected in it was Grandma Miracle, being shoved through the door by her livid son.

At the bar the old woman planted her feet. "Now goddamn-it, Leo, tell me what the hell's going on here or take me home where I belong," she said. "I told Bernie when I handed this place over to him I didn't ever want to set foot in it again and I meant it. And I hadn't, 'til you drug me down here."

"It's her," Leo said. "First she hired a no-good crew to replace the mirror—"

"You broke a mirror? How on earth did you manage that?"

"Then she won't even let somebody who knows a chuck from a bit keep an eye on the job. The least she could do would be to have her son down here, but no-o-o— she's got to have it all to herself. You leave it up to her, she wouldn't let a Miracle within a mile of the place."

"Leo, I *am* a Miracle." Martha said it as a weary concession to the facts of life in New Hope. Twenty-three years across the river and something had to give. She had tried to escape, but in the end the Inn proved stronger than them all. It had been here longer than any of them. It would be here long after they were gone.

"The hell you say." Grandma Miracle thrust out her sunken chest. Leaning on her gnarled cane, she crossed to the colored bar. "You're as much a Pickett as you was the day I set eyes on you. You hadn't done nothing but fight the Miracles for twenty years. Why give up now, when you got no reason to? Call yourself a Pickett if you want." She thumped the planks with her cane. "Turn this place into a palace. Or tear the goddamn place down and put in a hamburger joint. I hear that was in the works anyway."

Leo turned bright red. "Who's been spreading lies like that."

"Ossetta cleans my house as often as she cleans yours, only twice as good," Grandma Miracle said. "And I'd think twice before accusing a sweet nigger lady of lying, especially as she's old enough and smart enough to keep her mouth shut when it's important. Which is more than I can say for some of the people whose houses she cleans." She turned to Martha. "This place is yours, you earned it fair and square and if I can be allowed to say as much I ain't sure it was worth the price. But you paid the asking price and it's yours to do with what you want. Now Leo, get me back home and don't come after me with such horse manure again."

Already she was across the ragged planks that had tripped Martha up, that first time in the Inn. Watching her from the rear, Martha saw for the first time that the peculiar walk, the bow-legged Miracle strut, was not of the Miracles at all but was her own, hers and her six dead Blanchard sisters.

In the doorway Grandma Miracle turned and surveyed them

189

all, Leo and Martha and the work crew behind the bar, putting up a good show of looking busy and listening to beat the band. "I had forgot," she said after a moment, "the love that went into making those bars. Leo, get your mother home."

They left. Martha stared through the plate glass window after them, across the bottoms, plowed under now, showing their black earth to the sun.

"Ma'am," a workman said, "you mind if we have a beer? It's getting on to dinner."

"Oh, no, on the house," Martha said. She poured them drafts, one for each of the workmen. She poured a shot of whiskey for herself.

CHAPTER XIV

Answered Prayers

NO ONE EVER LEARNED who arranged the dynamiting of the Boatyard Bridge. The Fort Knox post commander told the Louisville papers he'd contacted the local authorities, who'd been eager to cooperate. The reporter returned to his desk and filed his story. The next day the men who lined up at the Inn's driveup window talked of nothing else. After they'd left Martha walked up to Mallory's to buy a paper for herself.

"But New Hope doesn't have any local authorities," she said to Leo. He stopped in every morning now. He never bought liquor or stocked shelves but only sat, following her every move with narrowed eyes. Behind tight lips his jaw worked. "That don't matter," he said. "They're going to dynamite it anyway."

"You act like you don't care," Martha said. "What if something goes wrong. We can't be more than a hundred yards from the bridge. And who decided we needed to get rid of the old bridge to begin with? I don't know a soul they talked to around here. I'd just as soon see it stay, myself."

"What makes you think it matters what you care, or anybody else," Leo snorted. "We're just people. They're the Army. This is a war we're in, in case you hadn't noticed. If they needed to dynamite the whole damn Inn they'd just come over and do it, and I for one would stand back. That's what happens in a war, in case you and your women friends never noticed." He unraveled himself and stood, all angles and bones against the bright square of sunlight. "It'd be no worse than other things I seen happening around here." He slammed the door and left.

It happened too quickly for thought. One day everything was normal. The next there were signs posted near the Inn's parking lot: *Road Closed*. Across the old levee the Highway Department erected bright orange sawhorses that fell over when the wind blew. Traffic was diverted to the new bridge.

That Thursday, the *Argus* ran nothing but news from the south end of the county. On the front page, a banner headline proclaimed the bridge dedication, scheduled for the following Monday. Inside, the Army bought a full-page ad: the bridge would be cordoned off to unofficial persons as of Sunday, three p.m. The Army would dynamite at sunset. No one would be allowed near until disposal and mopup operations were completed. People were welcome to watch the operation from the new bridge, a safe half-mile to the south.

* * *

Miracle took that Saturday night's shift. The Inn was crowded. The dynamiting was scheduled for the next day, the dedication of the new bridge would be Monday. People were in a mood to party.

Bradford Uptegrove was back in town. He'd shown up at

the Inn one evening, in full dress uniform and fresh from the bus from boot camp. He'd come straight to the Inn, without stopping to see Willie or Big Rosie or LaHoma Dean, living with her mother and five months pregnant with Bradford's child.

As near as Miracle could tell, Bradford was spending his days and nights at the Inn. He was there when Miracle replaced Martha at noon. He drank through the day. According to Leo, Bradford was there for closing at night.

He was going to 'Nam, as he'd learned to call it. Two weeks at home and then off to California, twenty-four hours to play in San Francisco, then across the ocean. He'd heard that in Vietnam women were cheap and the best dope in the world grew by the roadsides like chicory. He wouldn't be gone long, just long enough to kill some Viet Cong and make the California connections that he needed to set himself up on his return.

Bradford had changed, and Miracle tried to figure how. Louder? Bradford had always been loud. More sure of himself? Bradford had never been one to have doubts. But he clutched to his chest like his last drop of whiskey that part of himself that Miracle had once known well, that had brought him that Christmas Eve to the Inn to plead for help with LaHoma Dean.

More customers came, some with guests in town for the bombing. Cars waited at the driveup window. By the time the crowd began to clear, Miracle's head throbbed. When spare moments finally came, he found himself thinking on Rosamund. Her memory nagged at him with the persistence of the cockroaches that lived behind the pickled eggs. Just when Miracle was certain that he had his memory under control, when a whole hour had passed without a thought of Rosamund Uptegrove, he'd hear a snatch of Loretta Lynn and memory would scuttle from his mind's dusty cracks.

193

The driveup window buzzed. Miracle stuck his head out. It was Rosamund.

She was alone in Talbott's Mustang, her hair strewn about from driving with the top down. When she saw Miracle she half stood in her seat, reaching to plant a kiss on his cheek. He drew back, bumping his head on the window frame.

Rosamund sat back. "Come on, Miracle. It's not the end of the world. It's only getting married."

"You could have let me know. You could have written." You could have married *me*, he added to himself.

"OK, I should have let you know. I'm sorry about that. But what would have changed? You would have said don't marry him. I would have done what I had to do. We'd still be right here." Miracle pulled his head inside the window. Rosamund seized his hand. "Come on, Miracle, this is how your father would act. Be yourself. Do something different."

"Like what."

"Like giving me the chance to say I'm sorry."

"That's easy for you to say."

"You think so. You really think so. Miracle, you *know* me, a little, anyway. Easy for Rosamund Uptegrove to say she's sorry? I *am* sorry, Miracle. I'm sorry I didn't treat you better. I'm sorry I couldn't treat you better. What more can I say? I'm sorry I'm myself?"

Miracle pulled his hand back, gently.

"The bridge dedication is Monday," she said.

"I know."

"They've hired me to sing."

"Good for you."

"I hope you'll be there."

"I expect I'll be somewhere around."

She stuck out her hand, almost to the windowsill. He turned away, facing the long shallow U of the Miracle Inn bar, his arms

194

folded, his fingers working furiously, clenching and unclenching, picking at his sleeve buttons. For one miserable moment, he made this concession: letting something break, absolutely, for the sake of decency and wisdom, for the sake of this black-haired woman he loved. He turned around and took her hand. "Good luck," he said. "I'll buy your records."

She pulled his face down to peck his cheek. "I really am sorry, Miracle."

He pulled away. "You've been around me too much. You're starting to sound like a Catholic. Saying you're sorry for something you couldn't do anything about."

Rosamund gave a little toss of her head. "Well, it was *me* you all were after."

"Oh yes," Miracle said. "It was you." He lowered the window and turned his back.

* * *

The Sunday morning of the dynamiting Miracle rose early. He made enough noise to give Martha the idea he was leaving for early Mass. Instead he walked to the Boatyard Bridge.

He sat in his old haunt, under the north pilings, near the crevice where he stored his beer. A fat black garden spider mended the edge of the web she'd woven across the entrance to his stash. Near the web's center an iridescent June bug, the first of the season, struggled to free its wings. With one thin, jointed leg it grasped a nearby twig, righted itself, spread its wings to fly, only to have its struggles entangle it more completely, until it fell with an angry buzz into the web's center.

With a twig Miracle cleared the web. The spider scurried into the hole, dragging her prize. Miracle reached in the crevice and found the last of the last summer's beers. When he opened it, beer exploded in a foamy shower.

He could sit by the river for hours, emptying his thoughts into the slow flow of green ribbon, endlessly unwinding past. But he did not have hours. In a few hours the bridge would be gone for good.

And so would he. On his last sip of beer he decided: he would go, that night. The Inn would be closed; the Army had declared it off limits to everyone, even the Miracles, because it was too close to the old bridge. No one would miss him until Monday morning.

He took aim with the bottle. It shattered with a satisfying pop, scattering shards of brown glass. For the last time Miracle rose and climbed through the rocks and debris of the north pilings.

*　　*　　*

After Sunday Mass Martha walked along the old levee, past the *Road Closed* signs to the Boatyard Bridge. In the April sun the planks gave off the faint scent of creosote. Martha remembered that evening twenty-four years before, when on Rosie Uptegrove's dare she'd driven across the Boatyard Bridge to buy a beer from Bernie Miracle.

Cliff swallows darted in and out of the netting of cables and girders. She quelled an urge to return to the Inn for a shovel to dislodge their nests. They would die, Jessup County's first casualties in this latest war.

In the middle of the bridge she stopped. She squeezed her face between a cable and a girder and looked down to the water. She shared more than history with this bridge. They were alike, kindred spirits, always going from one place to another, never quite getting there. Not Catholic, not Protestant, not North, not South, not New Hope, not Mount Hermon, not Pickett, not Miracle. And what had it got the bridge, this constant journey? Eighty years of reliable service, only to

196

be blown to the sky in thirty seconds. The same might be said of herself, minus the fireworks.

"But I've got the Inn, and I've got my son, and by God I'm not giving them up," she said aloud, to the green water rolling by. She took strength from the thought. She stood on the bridge, her face squeezed between the girders, lost in her dreams, until the crash of glass breaking against concrete, somewhere below the bridge, startled her into life.

She walked back to lock up the Inn. Ahead of her, the girders framed the road, overhead the sky arched blue, and it was as if she walked down a long tunnel, the end of which was barely in sight.

* * *

They assembled at sunset on the new bridge, all of New Hope and Mount Hermon. Leo and Dolores were there early. Leo was anxious to poormouth his uppity sister-in-law to anyone who would lend an ear. Over Leo's objections Grandma Miracle came along. Her husband, her connection to the Miracle Inn, had been thrown from the Boatyard Bridge. For all she knew, it was the last thing in God's good world on which he'd laid his eyes. She would see it to its ruin.

Willie and Big Rosie came, nosing a path through the crowd in another shiny new car, this one a Lincoln as long and black as a hearse, with side pockets on the passenger doors where Rosie stashed her vodka. Willie parked smack in the middle of the new bridge, where everyone could see his car. The Uptegroves didn't get out but pushed chrome buttons to lower the windows and held court right there, with Rosie pouring little dumps of vodka into her Coke when Willie wasn't looking.

Talbott and Rosamund came, with the top down on the snappy little Mustang. Rosamund climbed atop the back seat like a homecoming queen, waving and smiling and flourishing her diamond engagement ring at the women who flocked about.

Bradford Uptegrove weaved through the crowd, wearing his uniform, his pupils bright and tiny as the evening star. This night and the next, and then it was off to Vietnam. He left LaHoma Dean standing at the railing and circled through the crowd, kissing women full on the lips with no more than a nod to their boyfriends or husbands.

Ossetta came with the few black folks, mostly as old as she, who had not moved to Louisville or Detroit or been installed in the cemetery. They made a place for themselves to the rear and to one end, where no white folks stood because the view up the river was not so good. They stood in a little knot, talking of the sons and now daughters, gone away to another war.

At the last minute Martha appeared. At home she'd searched for Miracle, only to find his duffel bag packed with his clothes and stuffed under his bed. She did not stop to think what that might mean, but rushed down to the new bridge. Once there she scanned the crowd for him, but at dusk it was hard to tell one face from its neighbor.

Dusk or daylight, it was harder now to tell who belonged where. Most of the Baptists gathered on the south end of the bridge and most of the Catholics stayed on the north, but the young folks met in the middle and talked and sooner or later some of the kids from one side ended up on the other. Martha pushed through the crowd, searching people's faces. She met Baptists on the north side and from a distance she saw more than one Catholic face to the south. More than one Catholic boy talked with a Baptist girl. Martha knew they were flirting, right under their parents' noses.

Martha Pickett knew, at heart, that if she had not crossed the river, someone else would have. If she hadn't stumbled into the Inn, another woman would have. The times sat on New

198

Hope like they sat on everywhere. There was nothing anyone could do to escape them. Somebody was always there to come along.

But she *had* come along, she had been the first to step across the river. Because of her, in some small way things would never be the same. She turned to the bridge railing to hide her smile, a cheek-splitting grin of satisfaction.

To the west the sun touched the top of Strang Knob. The shadows flowed eastward, swallowing hillsides dusted with spring green, pink and white patches of dogwood in full bloom, the dark uncoiling river lined with sycamores still winter bare, their trunks showing patches of white. The mountain's shadow reached the Boatyard Bridge. To Martha, surveying the scene from the bridge railing, the shadow hesitated a single long moment, while the rusted girders and cables glowed blood red with living fire; then night crawled east.

Talbott climbed onto the hood of the Uptegroves' Lincoln, and Martha knew something was afoot. Willie was protective of his cars, the sort of person to straddle the stripes when angle parking so as to make sure nobody got so much as a chance to dent his doors. Yet here was Talbott, climbing in leather-soled wingtips over the Lincoln's shiny finish as if it were no more than a piece of construction equipment. He held a microphone, wired to a box and battery held by a soldier in dress uniform. Talbott cleared his throat, quieted the noisy crowd. Watching, Martha felt the crawling in her gut that she had known at that bright sunny picnic where Talbott had stared at her with undressing eyes across the Miracle masses. She turned her back.

Talbott rambled a little, thanking the people of New Hope for bringing in a Yankee for this job that might have been done—"though not as well or as fast"—by somebody local. He issued a special thanks to the Army, to the politicians of the state of Kentucky and Jessup County, to the owners of the

199

Miracle Inn, where he and his crew had stocked up before and after so many long days.

Martha felt on her back the eyes of the men and women standing nearby. She thought to turn around and face them down with the coldest stare she could muster. She turned instead to the river's dark line of trees, the intricate geometry of the bridge cables and girders, the cry, growing closer, of a blue heron out for some early evening fishing.

"Through modern technology and the cooperation of the United States Army Armored Division headquartered at Fort Knox, we can explode the dynamite from right here," Talbott was saying. "And I have asked my fiancée, your own Rosamund Uptegrove, to throw the switch." A scattering of applause, whoops, wolf whistles, and the crawling inside Martha's skin became a sharp stab to her chest. She wondered where Miracle was; wondered if, so much younger and a man, he was hurting the same way as herself. Or was it so different, across generations and sexes, that they could never share even this? Used to so many years not feeling, then caught up in the storm surrounding herself and Talbott and Bernie and Bernie's death, she had never thought to ask this of her son, this boy now a man. She felt suddenly a knife of fear turning in her heart, the deepest stab of loneliness that can come only when surrounded by the most familiar people: family, friends, neighbors. It was that great guilt, come again: had she failed her son?—and it was more. She stood washed over by Talbott's magnified Yankee words, his narrow *i*'s and nasal *a*'s. She had only one bloody tie left in this town, and that was her son. She stood here about to watch the destruction of the link between the place she was and the place she had come from, and she had no notion of where Miracle was or what he was feeling, with Talbott's accent harsh on his ears and the picture of Rosamund climbing to the Lincoln's black hood fixed in his eye. She watched and listened and scanned the crowd for her son, while her fear and aloneness grew.

Rosamund smiled across the crowd and bent from sight. The crowd drew a single sharp in-suck of breath.

Martha thought she screamed. Many women did and men too, though Martha never heard one admit as much. In the same instant a blinding flash of light and searing heat struck the crowd. For a single second Martha saw all eight sections of the bridge silhouetted against the glare. Flaming planks floated high in the air, where they turned end over end in lazy arcs against the black flank of Strang Knob.

The full length of the bridge burned, until Martha could not tell where one section began and its neighbor ended. She stepped back from the bridge railing. Her knees buckled. Only the crowd pressing against her kept her upright. She took her hands from her ears, where she had clapped them with the first explosions. Above the pop and roar of the flames rose the first human sound, a cry that might have come from the dying in the wreckage. It came again, this time more like a whoop. It was Bradford Uptegrove, standing atop the bridge railing and letting fly his rebel yell.

The sound stirred the crowd to life. Another yell arose. In the red light Rosamund danced on the Lincoln's hood, her black hair flying. Talbott blew short blasts on his horn. North and south, black and white, Catholic and Baptist, the crowd screamed with pleasure.

Martha turned to look for the Inn. A breeze carried billows of smoke between where she stood on the new bridge and the old levee. She strained her eyes, shading her face from the fire's glare. She saw nothing.

Through the babble of voices Martha fought her way. She was not thinking but acting, now, from fear; and her fear was for the Miracle Inn.

At the bridge she hesitated, a single moment. Miracle was in this crowd, somewhere. The image rose to mind of his duffel bag, a fat, packed, olive-drab worm. She turned, once towards the crowd, once towards the smoke billowing between the Inn and herself; then she plunged north towards the Inn, onto the new levee.

The smoke roiled above her head, but a rain of ashes and cinders fell on her face and blouse. At the Y, where Talbott's new levee joined the old Jackson Highway, she encountered the roadblock. A group of soldiers sat in jeeps, guns at their sides, smoking cigarettes. Only one sat up in response to her request to pass. He was blond, with cheeks that glowed red in the light from the sky. "Sorry, ma'am," he said. "No passage 'til the fire dies down. Not 'til tomorrow morning, I 'spect." He spoke with a Southern accent, a deep South accent, Mississippi or Georgia, as different from New Hope's mountain twang as Talbott's Yankee voice.

"I have to see about the Inn," Martha said. "I own a piece of property out there, the tavern."

One of the soldiers laughed. "I thought I recognized you. You're the woman that runs the Miracle Inn!" He shined a flashlight in her face. She faced him, head on. "What's a little lady like you doing running a roughneck joint like that?"

"Selling booze," Martha said. "Something I'd like to do more of. Surely to God I can walk out far enough to make sure it's all right. What if it's on fire?"

"What if it is? This is a war, lady." The soldier turned the light down, along her legs. She felt her temper rising. She spoke in the most matronly voice she could manage. "It is *not* a war. At least not here. I could call the fire department if it was burning. *Please.*"

The Georgia blond swung himself into his seat. "Climb in,

ma'am. Just far enough out to make sure it's OK. No entry, even if you think something's wrong.''

Martha climbed in. They swung around the orange sawhorses and onto the old levee. She peered ahead, into the smoke.

They were on it before she saw it. ''Here!'' she cried, ''turn here!'' They circled the lot, stopping before the plate glass window. Inside, the green-shaded bulb above the pool table cast its circle of light. Miracle stood at the bar, his foot propped on the rail, his back to her.

The Georgia soldier leaned forward, peering into the window. ''Now how the fuck—beg pardon, ma'am, but we're under strict orders. *Nobody* is supposed to be out here.''

''It's OK,'' Martha said. ''He's my son.''

''It is *not* OK. If the lieutenant hears about this—''

Martha laid a hand on his arm. ''He won't hear about it, though.'' She felt his resistance. She laid a finger to her lips. ''For a daughter of the South?''

He grimaced, then grinned. ''For a daughter of the South. Only.'' She was out of the jeep and inside the Inn before he could stop her.

How long had it been since Martha and Miracle were in the Inn alone? Since the hot August night of the fair, when Martha sent her son after Rosamund Uptegrove and herself after Talbott Marquand.

Martha stood for a moment in the door, watching him from behind, noticing how much older he looked. He looks more like a Miracle every day, she thought, he grows more sharp edges. Since the summer he had pulled deeper into himself until he seemed to belong to no one. That, too, was like Bernie. Only his hair set him apart, that wild mop red as fall sumac, growing redder even than her own hair, as the rest of him grew more and more like Bernie.

203

She stirred herself. He was trying to leave, time was short. They were alone. She would speak of her plans for the Inn, of her love for him, how she had loved Bernie and Talbott, in her way. She would talk of how love worked, and how it didn't. She would talk of her love for the Inn itself, for this place that had been there before any of them, and that would be there after they were gone. "Miracle," she said.

He turned. "You're late," he said, in the voice that Bernie might have used to say the same thing. "I expected you here fifteen minutes ago."

"We can't stay away. The place won't let us."

"*You* can't stay away. I don't give a damn if the place burns to the ground ten minutes after I'm gone."

"So you snuck out here past half the U.S. Army just to enjoy the view."

For a moment Miracle said nothing. He turned away from her. "I snuck past the roadblock to have a beer for the road," he said finally. "I'm leaving."

She was not listening. She had listened too long, and what she wanted to say was too important. She had switched gears, from years of idle waiting to a headlong rush into her first chance to escape, and now she was back here again, with her son, her lover's lover's lover, and gearing down was not possible, not here, not yet. "It's time we had a talk," she said, moving to the bar.

"About what?"

"About the Inn. About your father." This was the hard part. "About Talbott Marquand." He stood at the pool table, rolling the cue ball from hand to hand across the green baize. He said nothing. "It's just you and me, Miracle, you and me and the Inn, we're all that's left."

"It's you. It's you, and it's the Inn. It's not me."

"We'll change it all," she said. "It's not going to be like it was before. I've changed things before. I'm changing them again. I'll figure out how to do it different and by God I'll make it different. Talbott and Rosamund—screw them both. They got what they deserve, which is each other. We've got what we've had all along, which is each other. We'll change how things are done and wake up this whole damn town in the process. We'll make things different."

Miracle smiled. "You do that. If anybody can you can. But I'm leaving."

"Leaving?" His words sank in. She rested a hand on the bar, for the feel of its warm, substantial bulk under her hands. "When?"

"Tonight. Now. It's what you wanted. It's what you've tried to get me to do for years. Well, you were right."

He was right. She had prayed that he would get out and away. She'd got what she wanted; her prayers had been answered.

She slumped against the bar, rubbing her temples with her thumbs. "Miracle, don't leave," she said dully. "Not now. We can change things. We will change things."

"You're saying that a little late, seems to me. If it's so easy to change things, why didn't you change things with my father?"

Martha clenched her teeth. It's the Miracle in you, she wanted to scream, but she knew it was more. He was a man now, his own man. He had turned into a man in this past year, while she was looking the other way. "You can hurt somebody you love, Miracle. It happens. If you love somebody, it happens. It will happen to you."

"Not if you don't need anybody in the first place. You can't hurt somebody if you don't need them and they don't need

205

you. It's the needing that makes you weak. So you just don't need, or you have the gumption to keep it to yourself. Whichever. You just don't let it happen, that's all."

"Oh, no," she said, from instinct more than thought. Then she heard the echo in his words. "Never a fool for love." She'd thought it herself, not so long ago. Coming from her son it sounded foolish. She had loved and been loved, and for all her regrets she knew better. There was no giving it up, any more than giving up the Inn itself.

"There's nothing there but hurt," he said.

"There's that. But there's more, Miracle. It just takes guts. You wear your heart on your sleeve and you expect people to take a pot shot at it and they do, and then you have a stronger heart. How are you going to know what it feels like to be run over by a train, unless you lie down on the track?" He laughed at this, a slow, quiet snort, as if he found it funny but didn't want her to know. Encouraged, she plowed on. "I have the guts to come down here because I love the place. I had the guts to love Talbott, to love Bernie; however, things didn't work out, I loved them both, in a way. Not a perfect way. But a way."

"I don't believe you."

The readiness of his words hurt, quick and deep. Him, too, a part of her cried. She pushed it down. You can hurt somebody you love, she told herself. He is a son. This is his right. She thought of ways to say this, to fit all the words she knew together to say what she wanted to say. In the end she knew only the truth, and could think of nothing better than to say it. "Oh, Miracle, I did love them. I wasn't much older than you when I met Bernie. Owner and operator of the Miracle Inn. Who wouldn't fall for Satan's bartender, when he offers you a drink from the devil's family heirloom? And so I fell, if it

206

wasn't love it was falling, I know that, I had no more choice in what I was doing than a coon on the run.

"And then I was treed, and what could I do but sit tight and make the best of things? And I did, and I had you."

The cueball slipped neatly from Miracle's hands. In the silence it dropped neatly into the pool table's north corner pocket.

Miracle stirred himself and circled the room, turning out the lights except for the bare bulb in its green shade, over the pool table. In his walk, in that bow-legged Blanchard swagger, Martha saw Bernie. There were things to say, things she had wanted to say all her life. She crossed the uneven floor to his side.

He pulled a silver flask from his pocket. "Satan's heirloom," he said. "Father gave it to me, Christmas Day. He said it's never left the hands of the Miracle who ran the Inn. He wanted it kept that way." He stuck its cool weight into her hand.

"Miracle," she began.

"I know," he said. "Closing time." He tugged at the cord that dangled from the pool table light. In the swath of blue light from the parking lot streetlamp he picked his way across the planks, leaving Martha alone in the dark.

She thought to follow him, to explain her mistakes. Words, words, words, surely she could put those into words, could teach him to love wisely, to avoid her mistakes and pain.

She made herself stand still. He had earned the right to go; she let him go. She stood back from the door, until she was sure he had enough time to clear the levee, until she was sure he was gone.

Outside, the Georgia blond sat in his jeep, drumming his fingers on the wheel. She climbed in. "Satisfied?" he asked.

The jeep jerked forward, throwing her back into her seat. "Beg pardon," he said, "but if the lieutenant happens along he'll be pissed."

At the orange sawhorses they stopped. He thrust his handkerchief at her. "Ma'am, I'm sorry to have to tell you this but your face is covered with gunk."

She took his handkerchief and wiped her face. The handkerchief came away black. "I'm sorry," she said. "Here I've gone and messed up your handkerchief."

"Uh-huh. Well, I guess you can get somewhere to wash up. You must live hereabouts."

"Very close. Not far at all." She gave him back his handkerchief, then seized his hand and shook it. "Thanks for your kindness. If you're ever this way again, stop in. Whatever you want. It's on the house."

"Thank you, ma'am, I appreciate that. We'll be around for the next few days. I just might take you up on that."

She was sure he was smiling, though it was dark and his face was turned from her. She climbed from the jeep. She was torn inside, she was hoping to see Miracle returning, his mind changed, all angles and bones and love and forgiveness. But in turning around, in looking for her son, her eyes strayed to the pale blond halo of the soldier's hair, as he drove around the barriers to rejoin the roadblock. She stood watching, until he disappeared into the smoke.

CHAPTER XV

Crossing the River

MIRACLE WALKED to the north end of New Hope before the new bridge cleared of people. After a while there came a steady stream of cars that during the dynamiting had been held back. He was afraid to hitchhike. The chances were too great that any car that stopped might belong to a friend of the family. He stepped from the road and hid in the woods. He found a patch of pine needles, not too damp, where he lay back, his duffel bag for a pillow, and fell asleep.

When he awoke the highway was empty. He stood on the gravel shoulder of the road for an hour, thumb out. Five cars passed, none even hesitating at the sight of a young man with a duffel bag standing at the road's edge.

He never considered turning back. Free of the place, free of his name, free of his family, free of the past, he was free at last, like a Holy Roller getting religion on the floor with God: thank God, thank God, free at last.

Just before dawn a truck stopped, a semi-trailer truck that took up its side of the road and then some. Miracle needed the driver's hand to help him into the cab.

In the light from the dash, Miracle studied the driver, his first accomplice on the road to freedom. He was thick, with a round belly nesting against the steering wheel. In one hand he gripped the wheel, in the other he held a cup of coffee and a cigarette. He wore thick black safety glasses that slipped down his nose. Every few minutes he pushed them up with the lip of his cup.

"You from around here," he said, after going through the shift pattern.

"Sort of."

"I figgered. Pour me some coffee. There's a thermos under your seat. Not too much, I got to be able to shift." Miracle poured. The driver took the cup without so much as a nod of thanks. "What are you doing here," he said.

"Hitchhiking."

"I can see that," the driver said drily. "You're not one of them draft dodgers, are you?"

"No, sir," Miracle said.

The driver shot a glance sideways. "I *see*. Well, I'm sorry but you can't be too careful these days. I don't have no truck with draft dodgers. I got too much at stake. Besides, they ought to be where they're running from."

"What are you doing here so early?" Miracle asked, anxious to turn the conversation from himself. "How come you're not on the turnpike?"

"Overweight," the driver said cheerfully. For a moment Miracle thought he meant himself. "Too many cops on the turnpike. Besides, I thought I might as well try out a new road. I ain't never been this way, you couldn't take a truck this size this way until they opened up a new bridge just south of here."

"I know."

"I reckoned you might. Well, they'll be barreling through now. Every overweight truck in Dixie'll find out about this road. Them turnpike cops are mean." The driver slurped some coffee. "Maybe you can tell me what's going on down there. I drove across that bridge and it looked like the flames of hell, just to the north, all this smoke and whatnot. Look like they blowed the place up."

"They did."

"Blow it up, eh? *That* must have been one hell of a sight."

It was, Miracle thought, it surely was, but you won't get it out of me. He was getting better at this game. He kept his mouth shut.

They entered Blue Gap, where the highway twisted and turned back on itself before shaking free of the hills and striking north in a straight line for Louisville. They rounded the last hairpin curve. The road cut a swath into a limestone cliff, then hugged a creek down through the hollow and out into the flatlands. Miracle craned his neck for a look at the knobs disappearing to his right. The first hint of dawn outlined the hills in darkest blue, darker than the Virgin's cloak, the color of Rosamund's eyes. Miracle pushed the thought from his mind.

"So I guess you're old enough to run away," the driver said.

"I'm not running away."

"And I'm a Christian man that goes to church on Sundays and keeps his eyes on the sidewalk when the pretty girls pass. That's OK. You ain't getting no shit from *me*. When I think what I left home. Where're you heading?"

"Wherever this truck takes me," Miracle said. "And then some."

"Well, I'm going to Chicago, and then I'm turning right

211

around and heading back to Alabama. You let me know where you want off. Hell, I could even bring you right back, you change your mind.''

''I won't change my mind.''

''I believe you. You don't look like the mind-changing type. Not with a jaw like that. My mamma told me once, 'A square jaw is a square deal.' *She* married a man with no more chin than a fox.'' He pumped down the window to spit his cigarette butt into the wind. ''Where'd you get a jaw like that anyhow?''

''Chicago,'' Miracle said abruptly.

''My ass. If you was born in Chicago, I was born on the moon. I can't say what family that jaw comes from, but that's family, sure as my shitty eyes. People around town see these thick glasses, they say, 'Eyes that bad, you must be a Essex,' and they're right. It's in the blood, and there ain't nothing you can do about it. Running away from that kind of thing's like running away from your shadow. I know. I tried.''

They rolled on. The sky lightened. ''Chicago,'' Miracle said. He liked the way it rolled off his tongue. It had a north sound to it, tall buildings and millions of people and baseball in July.

''It'll be cold as a dead snipe's asshole, April in Chicago,'' the driver said.

''I'll get along.'' Miracle turned to the window, to let the conversation drop.

In the sky, a band of rose widened above the distant hills. Traffic thickened. The truck entered a cloverleaf, the driver engineering the tight curve with much cursing and grinding of gears.

Then they were on the turnpike, heading north. Past downtown Louisville, a grouping of squat square buildings with a single framework of steel and blue glass rising at one end.

212

Chicago will be bigger than this, Miracle thought, bigger than imagination, stores and buildings and millions of people, not one of whom had heard the Miracle name or bought liquor at the Miracle Inn.

Then they were on the bridge across the Ohio River. Miracle looked down, miles it seemed, to the tugboats pushing flat barges, slicing the olive glass surface of the river. From his perch high above he looked back to the south, past the smokestacks and through the city's yellow smog, to the faintest line of hills farthest seen, where the sun poked between two rounded knobs. Through the haze, he saw the twin hills of the colored bar, carved in golden oak, with the vines and clusters of grapes to either side, and the sun peeking from rounded hills in the center. Leaning his head against the cool window, he closed his eyes and lost himself in his dreams.

* * *

Martha slept poorly that night. Bernie and Talbott and the blond soldier from Georgia and the fancy dancer in the mountain cafe all wandered through her dreams, sometimes changing faces in a way just the shy side of a nightmare.

At dawn she gave up the fight. She made her bed and straightened the room. The wood mosaics stared down from the wall, Mary Mother of Sorrows and the Sacred Heart of Jesus. Martha felt she had her own share of sorrows—lost loves, lost husband, lost family and friends—though she was lagging far behind the Virgin in getting publicity for them. When first she had laid eyes on the mosaics, she wondered if she would ever be able to accept her troubles with that patient saintliness. She knew now that she would not.

She did not check Miracle's bedroom. Instead she walked to the Inn, to see how it had survived and to postpone for a few minutes the certainty that Miracle was gone for good.

213

The parking lot was covered with ash. The windows were gray. To the south thin wisps of smoke rose from the charred remains of the Boatyard Bridge.

She circled the roadblocks and walked past the road's end to the river bank. A jumble of twisted, half-melted girders half-dammed the river, whose floating trash and brush wedged itself against the rubble. Where once there had been creosoted planking there stood only the stone pilings, marching like blackened tombstones from one bank to the next. Cracked and crumbling, they were strong enough still to hold the whole mess in place. "The first heavy rain and we really *will* have a mess," Martha muttered. "And where will the Army be then?"

She watched the river and the ruins: this place that had changed, once a bridge from one life to another, now a reminder of her wantings and weaknesses. She did not stay long.

Back at the Inn she glanced into the storeroom, where a fifth of bourbon had been jarred from its shelf, filling the air with the brown smell of spilled whiskey. She mopped up the glass and bourbon and opened the back door to let in air.

The front door opened. She cocked her head. Her heart beat a little faster; her face flushed. Only a stranger would come to the Inn when it was so clearly closed. Someone in town for the dedication, someone from away, from over the hills—maybe the Georgia blond, taking her up on her invitation? With spring in her step she bounded through the storeroom bins and boxes, toward the open door.

It was Talbott Marquand. He stood before the colored bar. He opened his mouth and closed it, once, then started again. "Where's Miracle?"

"He's gone," she said simply. "For good, as far as I can tell. For *his* good, as far as I can tell."

Talbott ducked his head. "I'm sorry. I thought he would be here. He didn't say anything to me about leaving."

"When would he have said anything to you?"

"We talked, once. Not long ago. About you. About Rosamund."

"How nice that you found the time. You've been so busy lately."

"I'm getting a divorce. It takes time."

"Not too much time to get engaged to Rosamund Uptegrove." He flinched. Her lips tightened in a satisfied line. He did not raise his head or move from the shaft of sunlight piercing the plate glass window. In the yellow light his hair shone soft and fine as corn silk.

"So he just left," Talbott said.

"He just left. Like others I could name, but with the courtesy to let me know."

Talbott's thick stubby hands wandered around the brim of his hat. Martha had never seen him this nervous. Watching the workings of his fingers, she remembered Bernie and Miracle, now gone; and the woman who many years before had turned her back, for good reasons, on another man. She remembered her words to Miracle, the night before.

"It was OK, his leaving," she said. "Everybody has a right to turn his back on somebody. Once."

"Even somebody you love?"

"Especially somebody you love. It has to happen," she said grimly. "It's the only way to learn." Then she poured two beers; she made herself do it. She set them on the bar. "A beer on the Inn, before you go."

Talbott raised the glass. His eyes avoided hers. "Here's to the Miracle Inn," he said. "May it sell booze forever."

She seized on the subject, anything to turn their talk from him and her. "Now that's a change of tune. What happened to the hamburger joint and the car wash you and Leo had planned?''

"That was then. This is now. Too many beers later. You get to love a place.'' He took a sip, then set the beer on the bar. He turned to go. Framed by the lintel, washed in spring sunlight, looking over the Jackson Highway to the new bridge, he stopped. "I came down to give him a message, to give to you. I'm sorry.''

"It's OK,'' she said, to an empty room. He was gone.

She slumped over the bar. For a long while she peered through the beer glasses at the Jackson Highway, watching the beer go flat, testing the sinking hole in her stomach. She felt its edges, how sharp they were, how big the pain was, how it had grown over the years, with Bernie and Miracle and Talbott. And she was left with the echo of her words, and then only with herself, and the Inn, and the hole in her gut.

She knew of only one way to fill a hole that big. She retrieved a bucket and an apron from under the sink. She filled the bucket with soapy water. Miracle's bar towel still sat where he'd left it, neat and square, good bartender that he was.

She worked through the afternoon and into evening. She had no reason or desire to return home. If she were to open the Inn Tuesday morning she had a full day's cleanup ahead of her. She got down to it. She could hardly count on anyone else, or anyone better.

In every corner she saw things to do, things to change, ways she would make the Inn her own. Light from the rising moon filled the Inn's east window before she lay down her mop and rags. Over a beer she surveyed her work.

For one night, anyway, she was satisfied, but she would not quit yet. She searched the storeroom for a hammer and chisel, loading them in a burlap sack emptied of the sprouted eyes of the last potatoes Bernie had grown. She left the Inn, stopped, returned. From the register she took the silver flask, carved with Great-grandfather Miracle's initials, her son Miracle's gift. She tucked it in her pocket.

* * *

Of the two sides of the river, the dead Catholics had the better view, a thought that occurred to Martha every time she climbed the low hill to Bernie's grave. The air was warm with the first hint of summer. The moon was nearly full. Below, the towns spread to the river bottoms, washed in hard white light. To the south the white concrete of the new bridge fairly glowed.

A few yards short of the Miracle mausoleum she stopped. From her pocket she pulled the flask and drank. She coughed, a loud harrumph, in the direction of the mausoleum. Satisfied that it was empty, she went about her job.

In the white night there were no colors, only shades of gray and the thick black of the shadows. The polished granite headstone reflected the moon's bright disk. By its light she read the engraved names.

FRANCIS BERNARD MIRACLE   1910–1967
MARTHA PICKETT MIRACLE   1922–
MICHAEL PICKETT MIRACLE   1948–

Martha knelt before the stone, her toes digging into the soft mound of earth. From inside the sack she drew a hammer and chisel. She placed the chisel's point inside the leg of the "M" of her name, and with care and deliberation struck the first of many blows.

The job took more time than she'd expected. By the time she finished, her arms and back ached. She left the tools by the grave and stepped into the mausoleum, to rest on its little iron bench.

The recess smelled of stale beer and cigarettes and urine. The moonlight shone through the gate's iron filigree, throwing its floral pattern onto the floor. Martha took the flask from her pocket for a sip. She rested her head against the cool marble wall.

The family would be up in arms. She would deny it—kids defaced the cemetery sometimes—but they would know. Why her name and not Bernie's, or Miracle's?

Why indeed? Grandma Miracle's name remained untouched, though she had far more right than Martha to remove it. She had lived alone more of her life than she had lived with a Miracle, any Miracle.

Things seemed simpler then, back when Grandma Miracle buried a husband and ran the family, when Martha Pickett crossed the river. Bernie Miracle had not been the first man interested in her, but he was the first, and likely the only, from across the river. It had been easy enough to go with him; just a simple matter of making him into the person she wanted him to be, new and exotic enough to satisfy her dreams.

Now the world, once so far away, was as close as the bombing range the back side of Strang Knob. There were no dreams, no mysteries anymore. You listened to television, and a war a half a world distant came into your home easier than the neighbors and harder to get rid of. The Mass was in English, the prayers set forth in the same words you used to pledge allegiance and call the pigs.

As for the dreams that had brought her across the river, they were as battered in the face of this new world as her hopes for her love for Bernie. Dreams had been easier come by, then, when the world was so far away that it lived more in her imagination than in her life, and it had been possible to believe that she could transform herself and her world with a move of a few miles.

She had lived across the river. She had had a son and a husband and an affair, as Big Rosie called it. She had learned, the hard way, the only way, the price of holding on to dreams: how much larger her eyes were than her stomach, how much grander what she had dreamed than what she might ever do. She had best take Big Rosie's advice: forget the hocus-pocus and get about living in the real world.

She stretched her arms above her head. She had learned all that and now she had more dreams than ever. She wanted to make the Miracle Inn her own, into a place only she could imagine and create and manage.

She stirred herself with her recollection of her resolve. If there was such a thing as the right time and place, it was now. She had a chance, again, to do something nobody had done before, the chance to blaze a trail.

She would tear out the driveup window. She'd clear a passageway through to the rear and install a Dutch door, with a window. Customers could drive around back and be served directly from the storeroom. Firmly and politely she'd boot Leo out. She'd hire a bartender to take his place; she'd put an ad in this week's *Argus*. She would take out the pool table and have live music and dances, give people something to do besides brawl and drink. She would draw people from the county seat and the new interstate highway and maybe even from Louisville.

She would open the Inn to women. She would shock them all, New Hope and Mount Hermon alike. They would all say it couldn't be done and she would do it. They'd all shake their heads and moan and grumble and gossip, and then they would fall in line and follow. Sooner or later they always did.

She rose, muttering to herself. "So what could happen—"

She left the mausoleum and gathered the tools from Bernie's grave. The sharp moonlight etched the letters of Bernie's name and her son's name. A ragged black hole filled the space where her own name had been.

With a clink of hammer against chisel she slung the bag over her shoulder and hurried down the hill. The gravel under her feet gave forth a satisfying crunch. Below her the river wound through the whitewashed farms and fields. Above, the jagged edges of the moonlit limestone cliffs cut like broken bone into the night sky.

Nearer the gate, a movement in the shadow of one of the larger stones caught her eye. She hesitated mid-step, torn between curiosity and fear. She peered into the shadow. A boy and a girl crouched, barely visible, their heads bent, one body wrapped about the other. Martha shifted the bag to her other shoulder and stepped quickly on. At the gate she turned for a quick backwards glance. The couple scurried hand in hand down the drive, towards the mausoleum.

Standing at the cemetery gate, she remembered her own courtship, in the Miracle mausoleum; and before that, to the night, so many nights ago, when she had taken a dare and struck across the ragged planks of the Miracle Inn to buy a beer. She saw the Inn as it was that night: its polished bars, one dark and opulent, one rich with light, and behind them the skinny, square-jawed man she was to fall in love with and marry.

The Miracle Inn door banged shut behind her. At the white bar, the two men playing craps raised their heads. Bernie Miracle lifted his eyes to the mirror. In the silent second before the men spoke, she heard the rattle of their dice, already thrown, landing on the gleaming mahogany bar.

THE END

220